DEATH OF A KINGFISHER

This Large Print Book carries the
Seal of Approval of N.A.V.H.

DEATH OF A KINGFISHER

M. C. BEATON

WHEELER PUBLISHING
A part of Gale, Cengage Learning

GALE
CENGAGE Learning·

Detroit • New York • San Francisco • New Haven, Conn • Waterville, Maine • London

GALE
CENGAGE Learning®

Copyright © 2012 by Marion Chesney.
A Hamish Macbeth Mystery.
Wheeler Publishing, a part of Gale, Cengage Learning.

Wheeler Publishing Large Print Hardcover.
The text of this Large Print edition is unabridged.
Other aspects of the book may vary from the original edition.
Set in 16 pt. Plantin.

LIBRARY OF CONGRESS CATALOGING-IN-PUBLICATION DATA

Beaton, M. C.
    Death of a kingfisher / by M. C. Beaton.
    p. cm.
    ISBN-13: 978-1-4104-4520-9 (hardcover)
    ISBN-10: 1-4104-4520-8 (hardcover)
    1. Macbeth, Hamish (Fictitious character)—Fiction. 2. Police—
Scotland—Highlands—Fiction. 3. Murder—Investigation—Fiction.
4. Tourism—Scotland—Highlands—Fiction. 5. Dysfunctional families—
Fiction. 6. Highlands (Scotland)—Fiction. 7. Large type books. I. Title.
    PR6052.E196D4257 2012b
    823'.914—dc23
                               2011044254

Published in 2012 by arrangement with Grand Central Publishing, a division of Hachette Book Group, Inc.

Printed in the United States of America
1 2 3 4 5 6 7 16 15 14 13 12

This book is dedicated to my Australian friend Rachael Schreenan, with love.

CHAPTER ONE

Where'er you walk cool gales shall fan
   the glade;
Trees, where you sit, shall crowd into a
   shade;
Where'er you tread, the blushing flow'rs
   shall rise,
And all things flourish where'er you turn
   your eyes.
               — Alexander Pope

It is a well-known fact that just when a man reaches his early thirties and thinks he is past love, that is when love turns the corner and knocks the feet from under him.

That was what was about to happen to Police Sergeant Hamish Macbeth. But on a particularly fine sunny day when the mountains of Sutherland in the northwest of Scotland stood up blue against the even bluer sky and not a ripple moved on the surface of the sea loch in front of the village

7

of Lochdubh, he was blissfully unaware of what the fates had in store for him.

The only irritation in his life was the appointment of a constable to assist him, police headquarters in Strathbane having discovered that the small police station in Lochdubh was an excellent way of getting rid of the deadbeats. Constable Dick Fraser was marking time until his retirement. He was a lazy grey-haired man, but he had an amiable disposition, and since he'd arrived in Lochdubh a month ago there had been no crime at all, which suited him very well.

Hamish learned that there was a relative newcomer, an elderly widow called Mrs. Colchester, who had bought an old hunting box some miles outside Braikie. During the winter, he had meant to call on her, but somehow the days and months had slipped past.

Dick was asleep in a deck chair in the front garden, his breath causing his grey moustache to rise and fall.

"Get up!" snapped Hamish.

Dick's pale blue eyes slowly opened. He struggled out of the chair and stood up. Most of his weight was concentrated on a beer belly. He was quite short for a policeman, dwarfed by Hamish who was over six feet tall.

"What's up?" he asked sleepily.

"We're going to call on a newcomer, a Mrs. Colchester."

"Someone killed the old bitch?" asked Dick.

"Why do you say that?"

"I heard gossip she's considered poison. Bad, nasty mouth on her and she's got two grandchildren from hell living with her. Also, she's right fed up because Lord Growther, who used to own the place, left Buchan's Wood, the prettiest part of the estate, to the town of Braikie. Now some lass on Braikie council has been appointed the council director of tourism and the environment and she's been running tours to the wood. She's renamed it the Fairy Glen."

"Where on earth did you pick up all this gossip?" marvelled Hamish. "You hardly move."

"When you're out, people stop by the hedge for a wee chat. It does not, surely, take the two of us to go there."

"Oh, yes it does, you lazy moron. Brush down your uniform. It's covered in biscuit crumbs. Let's get moving."

The house which Mrs. Colchester had bought lay six miles to the north of Braikie.

9

It was an unprepossessing place at the end of a long drive, being built of grey granite without any creepers to soften its harsh square structure.

The doorbell was an old-fashioned one set into the stone. Hamish rang it. They waited a long time until they heard shuffling footsteps approach from the other side of the door. The woman who answered it was squat and bent, leaning on two sticks and peering up at them out of sharp black eyes from under a heavy fringe of wiry grey hair.

"Mrs. Colchester?" asked Hamish.

"Yes, what is it? Is it those grandchildren of mine again?"

"No, no," said Hamish soothingly, removing his peaked cap and nudging Dick to do the same. "Just a wee social call."

"You may as well come in. But make it short." Her accent had been anglicised but still held some lilting traces of the Highlands. Somewhere in the Hebrides, guessed Hamish.

She led them into a large square hall patterned with black-and-white tiles. It was wood-panelled. There was a hard chair by the door and a side table against one wall. Apart from those items, there wasn't any other furniture, and no paintings decorated the walls.

"Drawing room's on the first floor," said Mrs. Colchester. She waddled across the hall to where a stair lift had been built. She climbed in, fastened a seat belt, and said, "Follow me."

The stair lift went on and up, smoothly and efficiently, stopping on the first floor landing. Light flooded down from a blue glass cupola up on the roof. She extricated herself from the lift and led them into a large drawing room.

Hamish looked around, wondering if she had bought the furnishings along with the house. There were several grimy landscapes of Scottish scenes decorating the walls. The furniture was Victorian, heavy, solid, and intricately carved. A large silver-framed mirror dominated the marble mantelpiece. There were several round tables, dotted here and there, small islands on a sea of rose-patterned carpet, bleached pale by the sunlight.

From the window, Hamish could see Buchan's Wood. A tour bus drove up to a newly built clearing which served as a car park and began to dislodge passengers. He swung round.

"I believe you are upset that Buchan's Wood, or the Fairy Glen as I understand it has been renamed, is not a part of your estate."

"Oh, sit down and stop poking about," said Mrs. Colchester. "Do you dye your hair?"

Hamish's hair was flaming red in a patch of sunlight. "No," he said crossly.

"Well, as to your question, I was upset at first but then that Mary Leinster called on me. She persuaded me that the beauty of the place should be shown to as many people as possible. She has the second sight, you know."

"A lot of people claim to have that gift," said Hamish cautiously.

"Oh, but she is the real thing. I have my two grandchildren staying with me for the school holidays. Charles is twelve and Olivia sixteen. Mary called on me last week and said Charles was in peril because he was going to fall into the pool below the falls. I know he can't swim. I didn't believe her but two days later Charles did fall in and, if it hadn't been for one of the tourists who dived in and rescued him, he would have been drowned."

"I think we'll take a look at the place," said Hamish.

"Go ahead. Are you as stupid as you look?"

Hamish blinked. Then he rallied and said, "Are you as rude and nasty as you appear?"

"Get out of here," she snapped, "and take that fat fool with you. And don't come back."

"After such a warm welcome," said Hamish sweetly, "it will be right hard for me to stay away. Come along, Dick."

As they walked down the stairs to the hall, they found two children at the bottom of the stairs surveying them.

"I gather you must be Charles and Olivia," said Hamish.

"Cut the crap," said Charles. "Is the old bat dead yet?"

"She is very much alive," said Hamish coldly.

"Christ, she'll live forever," said Olivia gloomily.

Hamish sat down on the bottom step and surveyed them curiously. Charles was small and thin with a shock of fair, almost white hair and flat grey eyes. His sister was a slightly taller version with the same colour of hair and eyes. Both had very white skin and thin pale lips and long thin noses.

"Why do you want your grandmother dead?" he asked.

"Because our parents say our school fees are too much and they are threatening to send us to the local comprehensive where we'll be stuck with morons and chavs. If Granny dies, they get the money."

"You're English?"

"Yeah, from London," said Olivia. "You know, where real people live, instead of, like, moronsville up here."

The floorboards above them creaked. "Here she comes," said Charles. Both children scampered out the open door and disappeared down the drive.

"Let's go," urged Hamish. "A little o' Granny Colchester goes a long way."

"I'm hungry," complained Dick. "She could at least have offered us something."

"That old cow? Forget it. Let's have a look at this wood."

Groaning, Dick heaved his bulk into the passenger seat of the police Land Rover. "You'll need to feed your beasties anyway," said Dick. Hamish had two pets, a mongrel called Lugs and a wild cat called Sonsie. He had left them behind at the police station. To Hamish's relief, both animals seemed fond of Dick.

"Just a quick look," said Hamish, "and then I'd like to visit this Mary Leinster. I mean, think how easy it would be to get someone to shove that child in the pool and then get a friend on hand to save the boy.

Second sight confirmed. No more arguments about the use of the wood from Granny."

They parked beside the tour bus. Hamish noticed that what looked like a gift shop was under construction. Mrs. Timoty, an old-age pensioner from Braikie, stood at the entrance to the wood beside a turnstile. "That'll be three pounds each," she said, "and five pounds for the car."

"This is police business," said Hamish, walking past her. They followed a poker-work sign with the legend FAIRY GLEN.

Sutherland's frequent Atlantic gales leave the landscape dotted with poor bent-over apologies for trees, like men with their jackets blown up about their ears. But there are a few beautiful glens and waterfalls, sheltered from the brutality of the wind.

Because of the proximity of the Gulf Stream, former Scottish gardeners had been able to plant rare varieties of trees and shrubs. A gravelled path twisted its way among the beauty of overhanging trees and great bushes of fuchsia. They stood aside to let the tourists make their way back to their bus.

Hamish, followed by Dick, came to a rustic bridge spanning the pool. The roar of the waterfall, which descended into the pool, filled their ears, and little rainbows danced in shafts of sunlight.

"My, but it's rare bonnie," said Dick.

"Shh!" said Hamish. "Look at that!"

A kingfisher dived into the pool and rose again, a fish in its beak, its sapphire-blue wings flashing. It flew under the trailing branches of a weeping willow and disappeared.

Large flat grey stones surrounded the pool. Hamish guessed the boy must have been playing on one of them when he was pushed in. If he had been on the bridge with the sightseers, then someone would have noticed. The boy would need to have been lifted bodily over the railing.

Hamish had a longing just to stay there, drinking in the peace of the place. But he was becoming curious about this Mary Leinster.

"I think we should go to the town hall in Braikie and visit Miss Leinster," he said. "Did the gossips tell you how Mrs. Colchester got her money?"

"Herself was married to a merchant banker. Before his death, he sold the place to an American bank and she copped the lot on his death. So the daughter and son-in-law, that would be a Mr. and Mrs. Palfour, are right cheesed off because they're finding it hard to make ends meet. He's a landscape gardener and owns a nursery, but it's this recession. No one seems to want their gardens landscaped. The kids go to a progressive private school, you know, the kind where they're allowed to express themselves, which translates into a lot of four-letter words and no work."

Hamish looked at his sidekick with new respect. He knew how valuable gossip was in any investigation. He laughed. "Maybe you're like Poirot, Dick, and sit in your deck chair and exercise your little grey cells. How did you hear this?"

"Mrs. McColl, her what is married to that crofter up the brae at Lochdubh, goes out cleaning, and twice a week she and Bertha Dunglass goes up to the house. When Granny gets a letter from her daughter, she reads it aloud and laughs her nasty auld head off."

A cloud passed over the sun. The pool below them grew dark, mirroring the flying clouds overheard. Although it was a windy day, the glen was sheltered.

"Let's go," said Hamish.

Braikie was not very large and would have been considered a fair-size village in England. The locals did refer to it as "the village," feeling that sounded, well, *classier.*

The town hall was a massive red sandstone building. Mary Leinster had secured an office on the ground floor. They were told she was out but was expected back at any moment. They took seats in the reception area and settled down to wait.

Dick promptly fell asleep. The rumblings of his stomach and his gentle snores sounded out a little symphony.

A small woman walked into the reception area and spoke to the receptionist at the desk and then swung round. "Mr. Macbeth? You wanted to see me?"

Hamish nudged Dick awake and got to his feet. The sun pouring in the open doorway was in his eyes and he could not see her clearly.

"Come through to my office," she said. Her voice had a gentle highland lilt.

She entered a room to the left of the hall and ushered them in. Mary Leinster took her place behind a desk and waved them into two chairs in front of it.

Hamish looked at her in wonderment. She had a heart-shaped face and wide blue eyes fringed by heavy lashes. Her hair was long and curly, strawberry blonde, and rioted down to her shoulders. She was wearing a low-cut green blouse of some silky material which showed the tops of two round white breasts.

Mary looked at Hamish and gave a slow smile. She had pink curved lips.

Hamish experienced a sudden breathlessness.

"What has brought Sutherland's famous police officer to see me?" she asked.

Hamish pulled himself together. Dick was gaping at Mary, his mouth open. Hamish leaned across, shut Dick's mouth, and glared at him.

"It is about the boy, Charles Palfour," he said. "I believe you haff the second sight." Hamish's accent always became more sibilant when he was excited or upset.

"I don't know if I have or not," said Mary. "I just had this premonition. It came and went in a flash. I saw the boy struggling in the water. I have often seen him playing down on those stones by the pool. So I warned Mrs. Colchester that the boy was not to play there. She didn't believe me. So it happened, ten days ago, just as I had envisaged. Do you believe in the second sight, Mr. Macbeth?"

"Hamish, please."

"Hamish then. I feel we are going to be friends."

"We have a seer in the village of Loch-

19

dubh, Angus Macdonald, who claims to have the second sight. You must forgive me, Mary. You see, before I met you I thought it might be a stunt to promote the Fairy Glen."

She gave a charming giggle. "Hamish, the place is extremely popular already." Then she grew serious and leaned her arms on her desk. "With the recession, you know, there's not enough work up here. Because of the popularity of the glen, we have been able to give work to wardens, build a gift shop, and bring money into the economy of the region. Now you must excuse me. I have a meeting."

Hamish stood up. Dick had fallen asleep. Hamish surreptitiously kicked him on the leg, and he awoke with a jerk.

"Here is one of our brochures." Mary handed one to Hamish. On the cover was a very good colour photograph of the kingfisher, rising from the pool, sunlight flashing from the spray on its wings.

Hamish desperately wanted to see her again but she was now holding the door open. He said goodbye and walked sadly out to the police Land Rover. He didn't know anything about her. Had she been wearing a wedding ring? He could not remember.

As he moved off, he said, "I wonder if she's married."

The sleepy source of gossip next to him said, "Yes, she is."

"How do you know that?"

"Oh, a wee bittie talk here and there. Her husband is Tim Leinster. He and Mary's two brothers are builders. Not much work around these days but I suppose they got the contract to build the gift shop."

"Now, that would be right illegal if she's giving contracts out to the nearest and dearest."

"No, it was passed by the council. They're the only builders in Braikie."

"Then why haven't I heard of them?" howled Hamish.

"They only moved up here from Perth last year."

"Why?"

"I suppose they followed Mary when she got the job. Also, they've done a bit of work here and there since they arrived and everyone says they're reasonable and honest."

That's life, thought Hamish gloomily. Romance walks in one minute and walks out the next. Why am I such a failure with women? He thought of how he had nearly proposed marriage to television presenter

Elspeth Grant; how he had once been deeply in love with Priscilla Halburton-Smythe, daughter of the colonel who ran the Tommel Castle Hotel, and how he had been forced to end the engagement because of Priscilla's sexual coldness.

Was he turning out to be one of those sad sacks, always doomed to fall in love with the unattainable?

He mentally pulled himself together. He probably wouldn't see her again.

When he got back to the police station, it was to find an angry message from police headquarters telling him to go directly to Cnothan where two stolen cars had been reported.

Hamish loaded the cat and dog into the back of the Land Rover. Dick was wide awake now and complaining bitterly of hunger.

On the road, they passed a tour bus with the legend FAIRY GLEN on the front. It seemed to be full of people. He reflected that Mary seemed to be a dab hand at publicity.

Hamish considered Cnothan a sour, unfriendly place, and although it was on his beat, he visited it as little as possible. One bleak main street led down to a man-made loch. The locals prided themselves on "keeping themselves to themselves."

He knew there was a caravan park and camping area outside the village and headed there. The missing cars were a blue Ford Fiesta and a Peugeot. He checked with the slatternly woman who ran the campsite to check for recent arrivals. She said there were just two, brothers, Angus and Harry McAndrews. Their tent was pitched out at the edge of the campsite.

The two men were seated outside their tent, cooking sausages on a frying pan over a camp stove. They were both skinheads, covered in prison tattoos.

"Whit does the filth want wi' us?" demanded one of them.

"I'm looking for two stolen cars," said Hamish.

"Whit's that got tae dae wi' us?"

Hamish looked around. Next to the brothers' tent was a large bell tent with the front flap tightly closed.

"What's in there?" he asked.

"Naethin' tae dae wi' us," said the one who seemed to be the elder.

"Then you won't mind if I have a look."

They both stood up. One reached down and picked up a tyre iron. "Get lost, copper," he snarled.

Hamish reached out, seized the arm holding the tyre iron, and twisted it hard. The man let out a yelp of pain and dropped it. His brother tried to run but Dick stuck out a foot and tripped him up. They cuffed both of them. Hamish then looked in the bell tent and found the cars. He charged both of them with theft. He phoned headquarters in Strathbane and was told to stay on guard until a police van arrived to take them away. To make sure the brothers did not try to escape, even though they were handcuffed, Hamish forced them down on the ground and dragged their trousers around their ankles.

He turned round to tell Dick to put the stove out only to find that Dick had served himself sausages on a paper plate and was busily eating them.

"You're a disgrace," complained Hamish.

"It's not as if they're evidence," said Dick through a mouthful of sausages. "These are rare good. I wonder if they got them locally?"

Back at the police station after what seemed like a long day and having completed all the necessary paperwork, Hamish retreated to the kitchen. From the living room came the noisy sounds of a television game show. He put his head around the living room door and shouted, "Mince and tatties for supper?"

Dick reluctantly lowered the sound, the remote control clutched firmly in one chubby hand. "What's that?"

"I asked you if you wanted mince and tatties for your supper?"

"Oh, aye, grand," said Dick.

"I'll call you when it's ready."

Dick threw him a pleading look. "Could I no' just eat my meal in here in front o' the telly? Just the once?"

Hamish thought wryly that Dick looked like a child pleading with a stern parent. "Oh, all right. But don't you start dropping food on the floor!"

Dick smiled and blasted up the sound again.

It wasn't as if the man was deaf, grumbled Hamish to himself. It was almost as if by jacking up the sound, he could be part of the show itself. "I've spoiled him," said Hamish to Lugs and Sonsie. "I've been happy just to go on as if I'm still on my own. But tomorrow, no more deck chair for Dick. He can come out on the rounds with me. Also, he'd better begin to do his share of the cooking."

He knew Dick was a widower whose wife

25

had died ten years ago. He seemed to have no idea at all of household work and had even on one occasion plaintively asked Hamish to show him how the vacuum cleaner worked.

But the man was pleasant enough, and it didn't look as if any major crime was ever going to happen again.

The morning would prove Hamish wrong.

He was frying up bacon and eggs while Dick watched a breakfast show on television when the phone in the office rang.

When he answered it, Mary Leinster gasped out, "It's me. Mary. Come quickly. They've hanged him! In the glen," and rang off.

Hamish erupted into the living room and yelled, "Turn that damn thing off. We've got a murder!"

CHAPTER TWO

Bonnie wee thing, cannie wee thing,
Lovely wee thing, wert thou mine,
I wad wear thee in my bosom,
Lest my jewel it should tine.
— Robert Burns

An hour later, Hamish Macbeth stood in the beauty of the Fairy Glen while the bane of his life, Detective Chief Inspector Blair, lambasted him.

"You daft gowk!" he roared. "You drag the whole works out here for that?" His boozer's face and bulging eyes swung round at the phalanx of police, detectives, scene of crimes operatives, press, and local television.

"That" was the dead body of the king-fisher. It had been hanged. Its limp dead body fluttered in the breeze. A thin cord was around its neck and then tied to a branch of the weeping willow.

"Sir," said Hamish, "Mrs. Leinster re-

27

ported there had been a murder in the glen. She did not say a bird had been killed. It was my duty to phone it in and come here directly. I tried to call you."

Blair scowled. His police radio in his car had been switched off because he had been listening to a CD of Dolly Parton. He was a fat Glaswegian, thickset, with thinning hair and a fat face crisscrossed with little red broken veins. He detested all highlanders in general and Hamish Macbeth in particular. He was delighted with the fact that Strathbane Television was filming his rant at Hamish.

Mary Leinster pushed forward. "It is all my fault," she said. "But this is a dreadful act." Tears like crystal ran down her face. "I phoned Mr. Macbeth because in these miserable days of police brutality, I knew he would be kind and I knew he would listen."

"You're that environment wumman," snarled Blair. "Well, I'm not going to waste time on a tree hugger. Piss off!"

He stomped off, watched by a busload of tourists on the bridge. Detective Jimmy Anderson threw Hamish a sympathetic look before following his boss.

After he had gone, Hamish made his way down to the willow tree, calling over his shoulder, "Come along, Dick."

28

"Right, boss," said Dick. "We'll get this perp."

Watching *Law & Order* again, thought Hamish gloomily. He sat down on a flat rock, took off his boots and socks, and rolled up his trousers. The water at the side of the pool under the willow tree where the dead bird hung was shallow and cold. He took out a knife and cut the bird down, then scrutinised the knot on the branch. His long sensitive fingers probed the bird's neck. How had the darting kingfisher been caught in the first place? Did it have a mate or chicks? Was it a male bird? Where was the nest? Even in death, the colours of the bird were beautiful: cobalt blue and orange chestnut and red-sealing-wax-coloured legs.

There was a great splash from behind him. Dick had slipped into the water.

Hamish turned his head and snapped, "Get back up the brae and dry yourself."

"Can I help?" asked a quiet voice from behind him. "I'm an ornithologist. Frank Shepherd. You may have read my book on the birds of Sutherland."

"Yes, I'd be right glad of it. Is this bird the male?" He handed Frank the bird's body.

"The male and female are very alike," said Frank. "But I am sure it's the male. I would

29

like to take the dead bird away with me for a closer look. I would guess that it may have been poisoned first."

"Can you find the nest?" asked Hamish.

"If you let me past, I'll do my best."

Hamish gratefully climbed back up the brae, wondering as he went which rock the boy had fallen from. The ones nearer the bridge sloped down into deep water, so it was probably from there that he had been pushed in. He frowned. Why had no one sent in a report to the police?

Dick was slumped in the Land Rover with the heater blasting. Hamish dried his feet with some paper towels he kept in the back and put his boots and socks on.

He went round and opened the passenger door. "Drive yourself back to the station," he said, "and change your clothes. Then get back to Mrs. Colchester's place and pick me up."

Dick set off. Hamish waited until Frank climbed back up holding the bird. "I found the nest," said Frank. "Dead female and dead chicks." He pulled a plastic bag out of his pocket. "I found these bits of fish. I'm going to take them to a pharmacist friend and have them analysed. I think the fish might have been poisoned."

"Give me your card," said Hamish, "and I

30

will keep in touch with you."

"What's happening?" asked Mary.

Hamish introduced Frank, and then blinked. He had an odd feeling of being drowned in Mary's wide blue eyes. He pulled himself together and explained about the suspected poisoning.

"You've made a great success of this glen, Mary," said Hamish. "Do you think this was just a nasty prank, or do you think someone was out to destroy your tourist business? The kingfisher seemed to have been a great attraction."

"I would ask Charles Palfour," said Mary. "He's a horrible boy."

"I'm going to see Mrs. Colchester now," said Hamish. "When Charles was pushed in, why was it never reported?"

"But Mrs. Colchester said it was!"

"I'll get back to you," said Hamish.

"I'm relying on you," said Mary. She put a little hand on his arm, and he smiled down at her.

Hamish said goodbye to Frank and Mary and set out to walk to the hunting lodge. He reflected that he needed new boots. His feet were hurting by the time he got there.

This time a woman in a flowered overall whom he recognised as Bertha Dunglass

31

opened the door.

"Is Mrs. Colchester home?" he asked. "And I'd like to see the boy as well."

"She disnae like to be bothered," said Bertha. "Oh, well, I suppose as you're the polis, I'd best let ye in. Herself is out on the terrace at the back. I'll take you through."

A stone-flagged terrace stretched along the back of the house, decorated at the front with a balustrade. On the terrace, seated at a table, was Mrs. Colchester. The children were playing an improvised game of cricket down on the lawn.

"What do you want?" demanded the old woman, scowling up at him.

Hamish sat down next to her. He could see his action infuriated her but he wanted to rest his feet. "It's about the time the boy was pushed into the water. Why didn't you report it to the police?"

"I did. I phoned Strathbane. Did they send anyone? No. All I got was a visit from the man who rescued him, no doubt looking for an award."

"Can you remember his name?"

"Some doctor from Lairg, that's all I can remember."

"Do you know that someone has hanged the kingfisher from a branch and poisoned the rest of them?"

She put a trembling hand to her chest. "No," she whispered. "Get out of here."

"But I want a word with the boy."

"Speak to him and then get out!"

Hamish rose and made his way down the lawn. The two children watched his approach with their peculiarly dead eyes.

"Charles," said Hamish, "when you were pushed in, did you see who did it?"

"No," he said. "I was playing on the rocks under the bridge when I got this almighty shove in the back. I screamed my head off. Some man dived in and pulled me out. I kept telling him and everyone else I was shoved, but no one would listen to me."

"There's another thing. The kingfisher and family have been murdered," said Hamish.

Both children stared at him and then began to laugh. "What's so damn funny?" demanded Hamish.

Olivia recovered first. "You police do see crime in the Highlands," she said. "I am here to investigate the case of the dead bird. What a hoot!"

"I hope someone pushes you both in the pool next time," said Hamish, "and makes a good job of it."

Their cackles of laughter followed him into the house. Mrs. Colchester had disappeared. Bertha showed him out. "She seems to have had a funny turn," said Bertha. "She's off to her bed."

Hamish sat on the step outside and tried to remember the name of the doctor in Lairg. He phoned Dr. Brodie in Lochdubh and asked him. "That would be Dr. Askew," said Dr. Brodie. "Nice fellow."

"Give me his number."

"A moment. Right. Got a pen?"

"Yes." Dr. Brodie gave him the number.

Hamish phoned and waited until Dr. Askew came on the line, then asked him about the rescue. "I went over to see this famous glen on my day off," said Askew. "It would have been cheaper if I had taken the tour bus because they do charge motorists a lot. I wasn't on the bridge. I was sitting down by the side of it, wishing all the tourists would go away so that I could enjoy the peace of the place. I looked up and saw them starting to move. Then I heard this splash and scream and saw the boy struggling in the water. I dived in and got him out. He was all right. To tell the truth, I think the child just slipped. I couldn't see anyone around, but then I wasn't looking."

"Have you any idea how anyone could have got close enough, unseen?"

"Not a clue. Everyone was looking the one way to see if they could see the kingfisher, so I suppose someone on the other side with a pole or something could have shoved the little horror in. What a family. Granny Colchester called the police but no one showed up to interview me."

Hamish thanked him and rang off just as the police Land Rover with Dick at the wheel rolled up the drive. Dick was steering with one hand and eating a large sandwich with the other.

He slid down the window and spoke. It sounded like, "ErrottagaeStrathbane."

"Chew and swallow," said Hamish testily. "What are you trying to say?"

Dick swallowed a mouthful of sandwich and then said, "We've got to gae to Strathbane. The big yin wants tae see you."

The "big yin" was Superintendent Peter Daviot.

What now? wondered Hamish as the superintendent's sour-faced secretary, Helen, ushered them into his office.

"Ah, come in," said Daviot, smoothing the well-barbered wings of his silver hair. "This is a bad business. Strathbane Television asked me for a comment on the death of the kingfisher. I said we had more important

35

things to do. They sent me round this DVD. Watch!"

He slotted it into a machine. It started with a presenter explaining about the death of the kingfisher and then focussed on Blair giving Hamish a dressing-down. Move to picture of beautiful Mary Leinster with tears running down her face and Blair calling her a tree hugger. After Blair had left, Mary Leinster made a speech, saying it was not Sergeant Macbeth's fault. She was so shocked she had reported the death as a murder. But, she went on, something beautiful had been killed, not only the kingfisher but "his wife and the wee bairns." Then she began to cry again.

Comments from the angry crowd followed calling Blair every kind of unsympathetic villain who had no respect for the public.

When it ended, Daviot looked grim. "This is a public relations disaster, Macbeth. I want you to concentrate all your energies on finding out who did this."

"Yes, sir," said Hamish, a picture of Mary in tears impressed on his mind's eye. "An ornithologist, Frank Shepherd, has taken away the bird and some pieces of fish. He thinks the birds were poisoned."

"Tell him he may avail himself of the

services of our forensic lab. Now off with you."

"If I might have a word, sir," said Dick while Hamish looked at his constable in surprise.

"Go ahead, Fraser. What is it?"

"Would your good self have any objection to me appearing on a game show on the telly? It's a quiz show, *Get It Right.*"

Daviot smiled indulgently as he looked at Dick. Perhaps if he had been as slow moving and stupid as Dick Fraser, he might not have risen to the dizzy height of his job. "I don't see it will do any harm. In your own time, mind!"

"Yes, sir."

"Think Blair's been suspended?" asked Dick as they settled back into the Land Rover.

"No," said Hamish. "That one could creep his way out of any situation."

"Think it was those horrible kids?"

"Too planned for my liking. That bird was hanged there to cause the most distress. What's all this about a quiz?"

"I didnae tell ye because I thought ye might laugh at me," said Dick. "It's the morrow night. The prize is a dishwasher. Just think. No more washing up."

"You hardly wash a cup unless I shout at you," said Hamish. "Oh, go ahead. Make a fool of yourself if you want."

That evening, Ralph and Fern Palfour arrived at the hunting box. Fern's mother was angry with her daughter. She said she did not want her peace disturbed and wished she had never invited the horrors that were her grandchildren. On the other hand, Fern had been born just before Mrs. Colchester's menopause. She had been surprised to find that she was pregnant at the age of forty-four. But her late husband had doted on their daughter as Mrs. Colchester had doted on her husband. It was only after his death that she began to find her daughter — with her politically correct ideas, her wimp of a husband, and her nasty children — unwelcome visitors. She knew that her son-in-law was in financial difficulties and took some bitter amusement from the compliments he heaped on her grey head.

She told them they could stay a week, but that was all. Mrs. Colchester had another reason for wanting them out of the house. She had fallen in love with the Fairy Glen. She liked to get out of the house at night in her motorised wheelchair and go down to the wood and sit there, drinking in the peace and silence.

Mrs. Colchester was from a remote island in the Hebrides and had a strong superstitious streak. She also believed in fairies. She thought the glen was really enchanted and resented the daily busloads of visitors. At least when the Scottish winter settled in, she thought, she would be able to have the place to herself during the day as well.

The following evening, most of the police and detectives who were not on duty switched on their television sets to watch that joke of a copper, Dick Fraser, make a fool of himself.

At first Hamish wondered if he could bear to watch the programme, but he decided he'd better see how badly Dick was faring and be on standby with a bottle of whisky to comfort the man when he arrived back at the police station.

At first, things looked very bad for Dick. Up against him were four other contestants: a professor from Strathbane University, a schoolteacher, a retired doctor, and a lawyer. How such respectable middle-class people could volunteer to appear on a television quiz show, and all to gain a dishwasher, was beyond Hamish. The one with the fewest correct answers was eliminated at each round.

To Hamish's amazement, Dick steadily answered question after question, until only he and the professor were left. They were running neck and neck until the quizmaster asked, "What kind of medieval weapon was a destrier?"

There was a long silence, and then the professor said, "A siege catapult."

"That is the wrong answer. Dick?"

Dick screwed up his face. Hamish found he was sitting on the edge of his chair.

Then Dick's face cleared and he said, "A warhorse."

"Correct. Mr. Dick Fraser, you are our new winner and the prize is a state-of-the-art Furnham's dishwasher." The voice went on praising the dishwasher while Hamish sat, stunned. How could a man such as Dick, with this fund of general knowledge, have remained a mere copper?

He got his answer two hours later when a triumphant Dick arrived back at the police station.

"It's like this," said Dick, cradling a glass of whisky on his round stomach. "I've got what they aye call a photographic memory. I've only to read the thing once and I remember it forever. I watch lots and lots of game shows. They're coming next week to fit the thing up."

"Where will it go?" asked Hamish.

"We'll need to take out that bottom cupboard. It's full o' junk anyway. They said they'd do all the fixing and plumbing."

"Man, how come you stayed a mere copper?"

Dick gave him a crafty look. "You ken Strathbane well?"

"Aye."

"Well, I wanted a quiet life. I didnae want to go to crack houses and brothels and what have you. So I just acted stupid. Okay, I'm lazy. But being real lazy is a talent. Sometimes," said Dick seriously, "it takes an awful lot of work."

And it takes an awful lot of work to get you to move in the mornings, thought Hamish, having to shake Dick awake as usual.

But Hamish, in his way, could be as lazy as Dick, so after a hearty breakfast they both sat in deck chairs in the garden under the profusion of red rambling roses tumbling over the front door. Villagers began to stop by the hedge, all praising Dick on his success. Hamish noticed that a couple of widowed ladies seemed to be looking at Dick with new eyes. Maybe they thought a winner of a dishwasher might make a good husband number two.

The sun shone down. They could hear the sound of Archie Maclean's fishing boat setting out with another party of tourists. Because of the cut in the fishing quotas, Archie had turned his fishing boat into a "trips round the loch" vessel for tourists in the summertime.

Hamish hoped he would do well but often wished so many visitors had not discovered the normally quiet backwater of Lochdubh.

He was wondering what to make for lunch when the office phone rang. He went into the station to answer it. But because the front door of the police station was jammed shut with damp and never used, he had to make his way round to the kitchen door and in that way. By the time he reached the office, the call had switched over to the answering machine and to his dismay, he heard Mary's near-hysterical voice. "Oh, it's awful. The bridge collapsed. Come quickly." He cut into the message. "It's me, Hamish. What's happened?"

"Oh, Hamish, a party of old-age pensioners from Inverness were on the rustic bridge when it collapsed."

"Anyone dead?"

"No, but shock and some injuries. My husband and brothers were there and got everyone out of the water and phoned for ambulances."

"Have you phoned Strathbane?"

"No, not after last time."

"I'll phone them and be right over," said Hamish, "although they probably know. A 999 call would go to the switchboard at Strathbane."

The cat and dog tried to get into the Land Rover but he shooed them away. "Go for a walk," he said. "Not you, Dick," he added as the chubby policeman appeared round the corner of the station. "There's more trouble at the glen."

Detective Jimmy Anderson was already on the scene with several policemen when Hamish arrived.

"Any idea what happened?" asked Hamish.

"Aye, the wooden supports of the bridge had been sawed nearly through. Someone calculated nicely that the weight o' a busload of tourists would make the bridge collapse."

"Someone seems hell-bent on scaring people away," said Hamish. "But who would want to do such a thing?"

"The only person to have registered any disapproval was Mrs. Colchester," said Dick, "but she seems to have come around

43

to the idea. Folks do say she goes down there in the middle o' the night tae commune wi' the fairies."

"Have you met Mrs. Colchester yet?" asked Hamish.

"No," said Jimmy. "I'm just about to go there. Want to come?"

"Not particularly," said Hamish. "She's fair nasty. But I'd like to see those children again."

Jimmy's blue eyes sharpened in his foxy face. "What ages are the kids?"

"Charles is twelve, and Olivia, sixteen," said Hamish. "They're the old woman's grandchildren."

"I can't see two young children doing such a thing," said Jimmy.

"I think anyone with a chain saw could do it. That's what I would like to search for. Any chance of getting a search warrant?"

"Not at this stage," said Jimmy. "Let's go up to the hunting box. Doesn't the place have a name — like The Pines or Liberty Hall or something?"

"As far as I remember," said Hamish, "it was called Lord Growther's place and after his death, Granny Colchester's place. What about the wardens?"

"There are two of them," said Dick, betraying his usual encyclopaedic knowledge. "Colin Morrison and his brother Tom."

"And what did this precious pair do before they got the job?"

"I think they were on the dole," said Dick.

"Not like you not to have researched their backgrounds, Hamish," commented Jimmy.

"I was waiting for the forensic result on the kingfisher," said Hamish.

"Aye, well, it came through this morning. Rat poison in the fish. Let's go. We'll take Policewoman Annie Williams with us. She's good with children."

"No one, Jimmy, could be good with that pair. Where's Mary?"

"At the hospital."

"Was she hurt?" asked Hamish.

"No, just off to comfort her tourists and worry about paying out insurance claims, although she might get away wi' paying out."

"How's that?"

"I don't know about the ones who come in cars, but the ones on the bus tours have to sign a form that says more or less that anything that may happen to them in the glen is no responsibility of the trust."

A cloud crossed Hamish's brain and he frowned. Then he mentally shook himself.

Why should Mary sabotage her pride and joy?

"Stop standing there wi' your mouth open, looking glaikit," said Jimmy. "Come on." He turned to the policewoman. "Williams, when we get there, see if you can have a quiet word wi' the children."

"Right you are, sir." Annie Williams was new to the force. She was small and plump with a riot of ginger hair under her cap and a dusting of freckles across her round pleasant face.

The door of the hunting box was opened to them by a tall man with thinning hair and a lugubrious face. He introduced himself as Ralph Palfour. He looked alarmed at the group facing him, made up of Jimmy, Annie, Hamish, and Dick. "What's up?" he asked.

Jimmy told him about the bridge and then said, "I am surprised someone hasn't at least phoned you to tell you about it."

"I've just got back with my wife and children," said Ralph. "We went down to Strathbane to do some shopping. I haven't had time to talk to my mother-in-law."

"If we might come in and have a word," said Jimmy.

He stood aside to let them past. "I think

46

Mrs. Colchester is out on the terrace."

A thin tired-looking woman was just descending the stairs as they entered the hall. Dusty, thought Hamish. She looks dusty. Her brown hair was sprinkled with grey, and there was no colour in her white face. She had the same flat grey eyes as her children.

"My wife," said Ralph. "Fern, darling, the police are here because someone sabotaged the bridge in the glen and a lot of tourists got hurt. Does your mother know?"

"I haven't talked to her yet," said Fern. "I believe she's out on the terrace."

Ralph led the way and they all followed. At first Hamish, with a jolt, thought the old woman was dead. She had that crumpled lifeless look of dead bodies that the spirit has left.

Her eyes were closed and her face had a muddy look. But as they approached, she opened her eyes and said wearily, "It's too much. The maid told me."

Jimmy introduced himself. "I would like to ask you a few questions."

The children were playing with tennis rackets on the lawn. Jimmy jerked his head at Annie, who went down to join them.

"If you must," said Mrs. Colchester.

"Do you happen to know if there is a

power saw in the house?"

"You'd better ask those wardens. They look after the grounds as well. Lazy couple. Their idea of mowing the lawn is to let some shepherd use it for his sheep."

"Where are the tools kept?" asked Hamish.

"In the old cellar. You can get to it down the steps along there. The door's not locked."

"Excuse us a minute," said Jimmy. He said to Hamish and Dick, "We'd better suit up first."

They walked to their vehicles to find their blue forensic suits. When they returned, Annie had found a third tennis racket and was batting the ball to the two children. They all seemed to be having a good time.

Jimmy opened the door of the cellar and they walked down the shallow steps, switching on the light as they went.

In the middle of what had been the old cellar was a workbench. Along the walls, various tools hung on hooks.

But in one corner, Hamish's sharp eyes noticed a power saw of the kind operated by petrol. He called Jimmy over. They crouched down and examined it. "It's certainly very clean," said Jimmy. "You, Fraser, get back to my car and ask the driver for a big plastic bag. I keep some in the boot. We'd better bag this up and look for fingerprints, and if there aren't any, well, it might seem, if it wasn't the wardens, that someone in this house is the guilty party."

When the saw was bagged up, they returned to Mrs. Colchester and asked her permission to take it.

"If you must," she said wearily. "But it won't do you any good."

"Why is that?" asked Hamish sharply.

She muttered something that sounded like, "There's no pleasing them."

"What?" demanded Hamish sharply.

"Go away," she said, leaning back and closing her eyes while her daughter held her hand.

"Mrs. Colchester," said Hamish, "I believe you sometimes visit the wood at night. Did you go last night?"

"No," she said, and repeated. "Go away."

Jimmy called to Annie, who waved a cheery goodbye to the children and came to join them carrying her cap.

Outside, Jimmy turned to Hamish. "I've got officers questioning the locals and the injured at the hospital. I want you to see Mary Leinster and ask her for the personnel files on those wardens. I'll send this saw back to Strathbane with Annie. Annie, did you get anything out of the children?"

"Not much. Only that their parents are short of cash and they're worried about being sent to a comprehensive. But they're just ordinary nice kids." She put on the cap she had laid on the grass when she was batting balls to the children.

Outside, the sun struck down with that ferocity you get in the far north of Scotland where there is no pollution to diffuse the rays.

"Gosh, it's hot," said Annie. "I'll just take off my jacket and cap for the drive back, if I may, sir."

She tried to pull off her cap but it was firmly stuck to her head. "Let me look," said Hamish, feeling under her cap and giving it a little tug. He stood back and grinned. "I think you'll find that those ordinary little beasts have put superglue in your cap. When do you think it could have happened?"

"Charles knocked a ball into the shrubbery and I said I would go and get it," said Annie. "I'm going back in there to tell the wee scunners exactly what I think of them."

"Leave it for now," said Jimmy. "The lab will get your hat off. I think nail varnish remover is the best thing. Okay, Hamish, let's get to work."

CHAPTER THREE

Up the airy mountain,
Down the rushy glen,
We daren't go a-hunting,
For fear of little men

— William Allingham

At Braikie General Hospital, Hamish was told that Mary had returned to the town hall. Policemen seemed to be everywhere in the hospital to interview the people injured in the collapse of the bridge. Daviot was evidently pulling out all the stops to repair the public relations disaster caused by the death of the kingfisher.

He went out and joined Dick who was seated in the Land Rover, reading a copy of *The Sun* newspaper. As Hamish climbed into the driver's seat, Dick held out the paper folded back to page three where there was a photo of a girl with simply enormous breasts wearing a smile and a G-string.

51

"Would ye look at that!" said Dick.

"Oh, put it away," snapped Hamish. "Do you never think what an awful time that lassie must have running for a bus? And think what it costs for those silicone implants."

"If I may say so, sir," said Dick cautiously, "you'd be married if you had a bit mair lust in you and a bit less romance."

"Chust shut up," said Hamish furiously. He was not about to discuss his sex life, or rather the lack of it, with Dick. Besides, Dick should have known that one-night stands might work in a city, but in the countryside, no matter how free and easy the girl might seem, her mother would soon be round demanding her daughter be made an honest woman.

Mary was in her office and seemed to have recovered her composure. But she looked taken aback when Hamish requested the personnel files on the wardens, Colin and Tom Morrison.

"Is that really necessary?" she asked.

"Come now, Mary," said Hamish gently, "you don't want to force me to get a warrant from the sheriff."

She turned pink. "I don't have files," she said. "They were both made redundant when that building firm over in Invergordon went bust and they came in looking for work. I needed a couple of wardens and so I hired them."

"No references?"

"I phoned the boss of the building firm and he told me they had been hard workers. That was all I needed. You surely don't think they would try to sabotage that bridge and maybe lose their employment if the glen had to be closed down?"

"We have to investigate everything," said Hamish. "Apart from Mrs. Colchester, was there anyone in the town who didn't want the glen made a tourist attraction?"

"Not one," said Mary. "They're all delighted with the success because the tourists stop in Braikie and spend money in the shops."

"Where are the wardens now?"

"Colin phoned me. They're both at the glen. They're waiting for the police investigation to be over so that they can repair the bridge." She was wearing a blue silky blouse, the colour as blue as her eyes. She leaned forward earnestly and the blouse dipped at the front, revealing part of two firm white breasts. No silicone there, thought Hamish, feeling breathless. "Will you be attending the funeral?" she asked.

"What funeral!" exclaimed Hamish. "I

didn't think any of the injuries was even serious."

"We are holding a funeral for the kingfisher and his family. Mr. Daviot said we could hold it in a week's time."

"Good publicity stunt," commented Dick placidly. Hamish glared at him. Then he turned back to face Mary.

"It's not my idea," said Mary. "A lot of people loved those birds and need closure."

"We'll try to be there," said Hamish, although he was cursing Dick for putting such a nasty idea into his head.

Outside the town hall, two small boys were standing by the Land Rover. They looked like brothers, having a strong family resemblance with their shocks of fair hair and pale blue eyes.

The one Hamish judged to be the elder said, "If we tell you something, will you promise not tae tell our mither?"

"It really depends what it is," said Hamish, thoughts of child abuse running through his brain. "I mean, if it's something criminal . . ."

"No, it's just that we was up at the glen the nicht afore last and we saw the fairies."

Hamish's face cleared. "And you don't want your mother to know you sneaked out at night?"

The smaller boy rubbed his nose. "They scared us, them fairies."

"What are your names?"

"I'm Callum Macgregor," said the elder, "and this here's ma brither, Rory."

"Well, Callum, what did the fairies look like?"

"Didnae actually see them. But they was sparkly lights and then a deep voice told us to leave. You won't tell mither?"

Hamish hesitated. Then he said, "Give me your address and I'll do what I can."

He took out his notebook and wrote down the address. The boys scampered off.

"Might be making a fool of us," commented Dick.

"Maybe. But I'm going to spend a night in that glen just in case."

"You won't be needing me," said Dick.

"Of course I will."

A cunning look entered Dick's usually sleepy eyes. "Now, sir, ye wouldnae want to be leaving those beasties of yours alone?"

Hamish frowned. He daren't ask his friend Angela Brodie, the doctor's wife, to look after them again. She had told him last time that she would not do it again because Sonsie scared her own cats.

"All right," he said. "But if there's anything, I'll phone you on your mobile. Make sure you keep it beside the bed."

Somehow, Hamish had expected Colin and Tom Morrison to be young or youngish men, but they turned out to be both in their fifties. Colin was small and wiry, and Tom was large and well built.

They seemed eager to help, showing Hamish where the supports of the bridge had been sawn nearly through.

"Say one of the children, Mrs. Colchester's grandchildren, that is, got hold of a large chain saw. Could they have done the damage?"

"I don't think they could. See, there was just an old rickety bittie of a bridge and we took it down and built that one. Got oak and the struts are teak. I can't see a couple of kids having the strength."

"What did you do before you worked for that building company over in Invergordon?" asked Hamish.

"Nothing else," said Tom bitterly. "We apprenticed ourselves to the building trade when we left school. Then after all these years, when it went bust, it was out on the scrap heap with no redundancy pay. Mary's husband, Tim, heard about us and Mary offered us the job."

"Have you heard anything about distur-bances in the glen during the night? Lights? Voices?"

"Nothing like that."

"But you patrol the glen at night?"

Tom looked a bit shifty. "Some of the time. But the Buchan isn't a salmon river so it's not as if we have to look out for poachers."

Hamish questioned them further, taking notes, but they could not suggest anyone who might have wanted to sabotage the popularity of the glen.

Hamish thanked them when he had fin-ished. He turned to Dick. "You haven't had anything to eat."

"No, and I'm right hungry."

"There's a café in Braikie in the main street next to the town hall. People seem to like to gossip to you. I want you to go there and see what you can pick up. I'll drive you down into the town and come back for you in four hours' time."

Hamish phoned Jimmy after he had re-turned from Braikie and asked for the ad-dresses of Mrs. Colchester's two cleaners. He wanted to talk to them away from the house.

Mrs. McColl was not at home but he

found Bertha Dunglass working in her front garden. She was a middle-aged, heavy, muscular woman with dyed black hair screwed up in a knot on the top of her head.

"Oh, it's yourself," she said.

"I'd like a word, Bertha."

"Come into the kitchen. I could be doing wi' a cup o' tea."

The kitchen was a shambles of unwashed pots on the stove and piles of unwashed dishes in the sink. "Sorry about the mess," said Bertha cheerfully as Hamish narrowly avoided slipping on a patch of grease on the floor. "By the time I finish cleaning the auld biddie's mansion, I'm damned if I feel like doing my ain cleaning."

She made tea and put a cup down in front of Hamish. He sipped at it cautiously. It was really strong and she had put an awful lot of sugar in it. There was a faint mark of lipstick at the edge of the cup. He hurriedly put it down as Bertha sat down at the kitchen table and they surveyed each other over empty beer cans and pizza boxes.

"Is Mrs. Colchester fond of her daughter?"

"That yin disnae like anyone. She likes tormenting her son-in-law by saying she'll probably leave all her money to charity. He's frightened tae get angry with her in case she does just that so he takes it out on his wife, telling her she's got to do something. Of course those brats don't help. Mrs. Colchester calls them the devil's spawn which disnae help matters."

"Why do you continue to work for her?"

"She pays on the nail. Cash. End of every day. Used tae get the money out o' the strong room."

"What strong room?"

"I'm no' supposed to know. It's near the terrace. She kept the key on a chain around her neck. I had a keek in once when she didnae know I was behind her. It's packed with things of silver and gold, ornaments, plates, that sort of thing. It's said that old man Colchester was a great collector o' gold and silver. But she's given the key to the bank tae keep for safety."

Hamish looked uneasy. "I don't remember seeing signs of a burglar alarm."

"Her daughter's finally made herself see sense, and the men are coming next week to install a security system."

"What do you make of Mary Leinster?"

"Oh, her? One o' them green people, always wanting to save the earth. Mind you, what she did wi' that glen has brought in a fair bit of work."

"Wasn't there any protest about her giving the building work to her husband and her brothers?"

"Not that I heard. It was put up to the council and they passed it. O' course, Barry McQueen, the new provost, is right sweet on her. She makes sure o' that."

"Perhaps she doesn't have to," said Hamish defensively. "She's right pretty."

"Aye, and doesn't she just know it."

Jealous old bitch, thought Hamish.

"Did Mary Leinster just turn up one day and suggest that job for herself?"

"I think she came wi' some letter of introduction from some banker in Perth who knows McQueen. The council decided to give her a try."

Hamish thanked her and left. He then found Mrs. Greta McColl at home but in contrast with the garrulous Bertha, she folded her already thin lips into a tight line and said she did not believe in talking about employers. Furthermore, she didn't like nosy policemen. She'd heard about Hamish Macbeth. He was a womaniser and she couldnae stand men like that and good day to ye!

Hamish drove to the café where he had left Dick. Dick was deep in gossip with two women. He decided to leave him for a bit and drove out to the shore road and parked. A great seawall had been built to keep out the increasing height of the tides. He climbed up on top of the wall. A stiff wind was blowing from the west. The tide was coming in, great Atlantic breakers thundering up the shore bringing in long strands of seaweed that seemed to clutch at the sand like fingers. Along to the left where cliffs reared up, he could see gulls on the ledges, and far out to the west a dark line of cloud.

The weather's breaking at last, thought Hamish. I hope it holds off. I don't want to get soaked at the glen. He stayed where he was, comforted as always by the heaving fury of the ocean, until, glancing at his watch, he realised it was time to fetch Dick.

"So what did you find out?" asked Hamish as he drove them back to Lochdubh.

"A bittie here and there," said Dick. "Mrs. Colchester prefers her own company and is annoyed at having the family stay and says she can't wait to see the back of them. She keeps them all in line by hinting if they don't wait on her hand and foot, she'll leave her money elsewhere. Ralph Palfour had a big row with his wife the other night. She says, that's Fern Palfour, that the nursery he owns in London is in Fulham and on a prime bit of real estate and if he sold it, they could get a fortune. Himself shouts back it's been in his family for generations. She told him to do something nasty with his family and he slapped her. She burst into tears. He's been saying sorry ever since but she says she hates him. No wonder the kids are so horrible."

"How did you get all this juicy gossip?"

"Sue McColl, the cleaner's daughter."

"My, my. And that's the woman who's just told me she never gossips. I don't like this, Dick. You mean there might be a murder?" said Hamish.

"Naw. I mean the daughter and son-in-law would be prime suspects. They'll be off south in a few days' time and that'll be that."

"Did the women you spoke to have any idea of who might have sabotaged the bridge and killed the kingfisher?"

"They think it's some of the local louts."

"Like who?"

"Like a character called Ginger Stuart. Lives up on the council estate. Young tearaway. Did a stretch for pushing drugs."

"We'll call on him tomorrow."

When Hamish had written up his reports, made supper, and fed his pets, he took Sonsie and Lugs out for a walk. From inside the police station came the blare of another game show.

The Currie sisters approached him, and he paused by the wall overlooking the loch. Jessie and Nessie Currie were twin sisters, still called spinsters in a PC age which had made the word unfashionable. They both had thick glasses and tightly permed white hair.

"Do you think black would be suitable?" asked Nessie.

"Suitable," echoed the Greek chorus that was her sister.

"What for?" asked Hamish.

"The funeral o' the dead birdie."

Hamish as usual blocked out Jessie's sotto voce repetitions.

"I don't think so," he said.

"Why?"

"Bit over the top," said Hamish. "Maybe brown."

"That might do," said Nessie. "We've got our camel coats."

They moved on, arm in arm. Their place was taken by Mrs. Wellington, the minister's wife, who despite the mugginess of the evening was dressed in tweed with a felt hat crammed down on her large head.

"It's got to be stopped," she said. "A funeral for dead birds! Sacrilegious, that's what it is!"

"What about all creatures great and

small?" asked Hamish.

"I told my husband not to conduct the service, but he says it is expected of him. Heathen, pagan rubbish."

On the following morning, Hamish and Dick with Lugs and Sonsie in the back of the Land Rover set out to interview Ginger Stuart. This is why they call the police "plods," thought Hamish. One fruitless interview after another. Let's hope this Ginger has something useful to say.

At first sight, it was a puzzle how Ginger had received his nickname. He was in his thirties with a completely bald head and a thick muscular body stripped to the waist showing prison tattoos on his arms. He was tinkering with a motorbike in his weedy front garden.

The front gate was lying on its side. Hamish followed by Dick walked into the garden. "I've got bugger-all tae say to ye," said Ginger.

Hamish sighed. "Full name, or I'll have you in a cell for the night for obstructing the police in their enquiries."

"Walter Stuart."

"Do you know anything about what's been going on at Buchan's Wood?"

"Me? Naw. Never go near the place."

"Have you heard of anyone in Braikie who might possibly have sabotaged that bridge?"

He scratched his bald head. "Nope. I'm clean. The ones I used tae know, well, what's in it for them? They're only interested in any crime that pays for drug money."

Hamish handed over his card. "If you hear anything, let me know."

"Would there be money in it for me?"

"Sure," said Hamish.

"Right, boss. I know things about them streets what you don't."

Bless films and television, thought Hamish. He could see Ginger's eyes narrowing and darting here and there as he tried to emulate a TV tough guy.

The rest of the day produced very little. Dick had given up and had fallen asleep in the passenger seat with Sonsie draped across his lap like a fur blanket. Hamish wondered how he could bear the heat. The wind had suddenly dropped. It was one of those close, grey days where the highland midges were out biting in force. He rubbed his face, neck and hands with repellent and looked at the sky.

If it rained that evening, he was going to have a miserable watch.

But Sutherland went in for one of its dra-

65

matic changes of weather. A light breeze was blowing as he set out. He did not take a tent or sleeping bag because he only planned to stay in the Fairy Glen for an hour.

It was two in the morning when he entered the dark depths of the glen and made his way to the pool under the bridge. He sat down on a flat stone and waited. He could sense nothing but peace. There was the sound of the waterfall and the occasional rustle in the undergrowth of some small animal. Fairies, according to highland superstition, were not glittery little things but small dark men. But the boys had seen something and then a voice warning them off. As far as he could gather, the wardens were nowhere around.

He gave it an hour and a half and then returned to Lochdubh. An idea suddenly struck him as he was serving Dick breakfast. "Did you tell anyone I was going to be in the glen last night?"

"I might have said something to the Currie sisters."

Hamish groaned. "That's as good as taking out a full-page advertisement in the local paper. Don't you see that everyone would soon know I was going to be there? No wonder nothing happened."

Dick placidly chomped a large sausage.

"Och, well, all ye have to do is go again and I won't say a word."

Hamish's hazel eyes narrowed. "No, my friend, you'll go the next time."

"It's no' suitable for a man o' my years. I think I have the rheumatism."

"I think you've got the laziness. You'll go when I tell you to go."

The rest of the week passed in dreary police work, until Hamish felt he must have interviewed the whole of Braikie. He longed to see Mary again, but kept away, reminding himself that she was married.

The evening before the funeral of the kingfishers, Jimmy Anderson turned up with a thick file of papers. "Statements and more statements," he said. "Go through them, Hamish, and see if you can pick anything out we might have missed. The bridge is repaired and there's going to be a big crowd tomorrow. Lot o' daft rubbish. Do you think Mary Leinster is right in the head?"

"She's a good publicist," said Hamish. "A lot of the press are going to be there and the weather forecast's good."

"I'm surprised Mr. Wellington's going along with this farce."

"I don't think our minister realises what a circus it's going to be. Even a funeral for birds means whisky to the locals. There'll be a right party."

"The criminals down in Strathbane are rejoicing," said Jimmy. "Daviot sees it all as a big public relations exercise for the police. Going to be lots of us standing around like tumshies."

"Where are they burying the creatures?"

"Get this! They're burning the birds in the car park and then Mary carries the ashes in a wee box down to the bridge and chucks the ashes in the pool. There's a choir and a piper. Got any whisky?"

Hamish started to say no but Dick was already bringing down a bottle out of a kitchen cupboard.

"Well, here's to tomorrow," said Jimmy.

"Is Blair going to be there?"

"Daviot thought it would be more diplomatic to leave him behind."

Hamish grinned. "This funeral might be fun after all."

"What on earth is that noise?" demanded Jimmy.

"It's Dick's new dishwasher. I try to tell him to leave it till it's full but he's like a bairn wi' a new toy."

CHAPTER FOUR

The padre said, "Whatever have you been
and gone and done?"
— Sir William Gilbert

Although Hamish mourned the loss of such
beautiful birds as the kingfishers, he could
not help feeling there was something dis-
tasteful about the whole circus of the
funeral. He found he did not find it funny
at all. The Church of Scotland is well known
for its charity in believing that everyone
should be entitled to a Christian burial, but
Mr. Wellington, the minister of Lochdubh,
hearing he had been chosen because no
preacher in Braikie wanted to be involved,
and, further learning of the funeral pyre,
dug his heels in and refused to attend.

The enterprising Mary had discovered
there was a small commune on South Rona
called The Children of God and had persuaded the head of the cult, a weedy man

69

called David Cunningham, to perform the service.

Cunningham arrived dressed in white robes covered in silver tinsel stars. Hamish was sure the stars had been made out of kitchen aluminium foil. Cunningham had a long ponytail down his back to compensate for the fact that he was nearly bald in front.

The day was fine and sunny. Crowds had gathered around a small funeral pyre in the car park. Mary was wearing a pretty, flowery dress which floated around her pocket-size Venus of a body. She approached Hamish. "How you must be hating this," she said.

"As a matter of fact I am," said Hamish. "I'm surprised at you, Mary."

"I'm a businesswoman, Hamish, and it takes something like this to save the glen. Jobs are at stake. Think of the money the local shops make from the tourists. Have you ever known tourists bothering to visit Braikie before?"

"Well, I know, but it all seems a bit sacrilegious."

She sighed. "Just look on it as a party. Television's here. We even have no less a person than Elspeth Grant."

Hamish's heart gave a jolt. "Where?"

"Just arrived. Getting out of that Winnebago over there."

70

"Excuse me, Mary," said Hamish hurriedly.

She caught his arm. "Hamish, why don't we have dinner one evening?"

Mary's blue eyes were opened to their widest as she looked up at him. Her lashes were black and tinged at the edged with gold. He had a sudden feeling of breathlessness. "That would be grand," he said cautiously. "You and your husband?"

"Tim and I are getting a divorce."

"Why?"

Those beautiful eyes filled with tears. "I'll tell you over dinner."

"What about this evening?" asked Hamish. "There's a good Italian restaurant in Lochdubh."

"I'd like that. Shall we say eight o'clock?"

"Fine. I'll be there."

Elspeth was now in the middle of making a commentary. Cunningham raised his long skinny arms to the heavens. "Oh, God on high," he intoned, "bless these poor wee birdies and take them to Thy bosom where they may sit with the Lamb."

Bollocks! thought Hamish sourly as Cunningham droned on and on. At last he got to "Amen."

Two schoolgirls approached the pyre,

which was in fact a charcoal barbecue, carrying a white cardboard box with a gold cross painted on top of it. The Braikie Ladies' Choir burst into a rendering of "Amazing Grace," their voices nearly drowned out by a piper.

The box was placed on the charcoal over a metal tray, where it burst into flames. Cunningham began to dance around the "pyre" chanting in tongues. He was wearing open-toed leather sandals.

The choir at last fell silent and the pipes died away with a final wail. Cunningham danced on.

And then at the back of the crowd, someone burst out laughing. Soon, it seemed as if the whole crowd had fallen helpless with laughter. Cunningham stopped cavorting and glared. The laughter grew louder. He gathered his robes around him and stalked off.

Mary marched forward and nodded to the two wardens who, with gloved hands, retrieved the tray of ashes.

The crowd, now in party mood, followed Mary and the wardens into the glen and onto the repaired bridge. She solemnly scattered the ashes over the bridge into the water. She raised her voice. "The ladies of Braikie have supplied refreshments in the car park."

Everyone scrambled back to the car park, where tables of food had been laid out. There was even a refreshment tent.

Hamish found himself accosted by Elspeth. "Going to make a fool of it?" he asked.

"Not me," said Elspeth. "Not with a country full of bird and animal lovers. But, Hamish, couldn't you have found a way to persuade them to do something a bit more dignified?"

"It's all the work of Mary Leinster," said Hamish. "She's passionate about bringing trade into Braikie, and the glen seems a good way of doing it. You look different."

Elspeth's normally no-colour frizzy hair had been straightened and highlighted. Her face was carefully made up for the cameras. Only those silvery Gypsy eyes of hers seemed familiar.

"You know how it is, Hamish. Can you think of a plain-looking woman presenter? The men can be fat and old, but not the women. I've already picked up rumours that the glen is haunted by fairies. Looks more like it's being haunted by saboteurs. Who doesn't want an interest in the place?"

"Can't find anyone except perhaps Mrs. Colchester, who lives at the old hunting box. Mind you, she's got two hellish grand-children, but I can't see either of them having the power to wield a chain saw."

"I'll go and pay her a visit," said Elspeth. "Why don't we have dinner tonight and talk it over?"

"I've already agreed to have dinner with Mary Leinster," said Hamish, "but come along as well."

"Quite beautiful, isn't she? Married?"

"Yes," said Hamish stiffly. "So you wouldn't be butting in on a date."

"Okay. What time?"

"Eight o'clock. The Italian place."

"I'll see you there."

Hamish sent Dick off to pick up gossip and then walked down into the glen and leaned on the bridge. Everyone was in the car park, eating and drinking. It really was a beautiful spot, he thought. The peaty water of the pool glowed with a golden light. A fuchsia bush leaned over the water, its blood-red blossoms looking down at their reflection.

He felt he should not have asked Elspeth to join them for dinner. Mary had said she would tell him about her divorce. Perhaps her husband had turned against her and wanted to sabotage her pet project. He decided to put Elspeth off and arrange to see her on the following day.

But when he went back to the car park, it was to be told by Dick that the television crew had moved on to interview Mrs. Colchester.

He and Dick drove up to the hunting box. Once more the front door stood open.

"They should be a wee bit more careful," said Dick. "Anyone could walk in."

The television van was parked on the drive outside. They walked into the house and followed the sound of voices.

Out on the terrace, Mrs. Colchester was giving an interview. "No, I did not go to the funeral," she was saying, "nor would I let any of my family be a part of such non-sense."

"I believe you are against the glen being made into a tourist attraction," said Elspeth.

"On the contrary, I am very much for it. I am all for helping the townspeople find work. But I do not hold with funerals for birds. Such rubbish. Do you know I was told that I would make the fairies angry if I did not go?"

"Who told you that?" asked Hamish walking forward.

"Get out of the shot!" howled the camera-man.

"I can't remember," said Mrs. Colchester.

"And you" . . . she glared at the cameraman . . . "will refrain from giving orders on my property."

The two grandchildren, Olivia and Charles, were sitting on the ground beside her, looking up at her with adoring expressions. Ralph and Fern Palfour were standing a little to one side, gazing fondly on the scene.

It all looked like a television soap to Hamish.

"And I'm tired," said Mrs. Colchester. "Shove off, the lot of you. Fern, help me inside, dear."

"Yes, Mother. Of course, Mother."

With Fern on one side of her and Ralph on the other, she went inside to her stair lift and buckled herself in. Hamish had followed her in.

"You," she said to him. "Come back tomorrow. I've decided to tell you something."

"Can't you tell me now?"

"No. This lot will be away by tomorrow. I don't want them hearing what I have to say."

She started the stair lift and glided smoothly upwards.

Hamish went back out to the terrace to join Elspeth. "I can't join you this evening," she said. "I've been summoned back. It's all these price cuts. If anything happens, Hamish, follow the money."

"What do you mean?"

"Mrs. Colchester is worth millions. Her son-in-law is nearly bankrupt. I feel something bad about this place."

Dick said, "I don't think anyone'll try anything again. A lot of the townspeople are forming a Protect Our Glen squad. They're going to patrol it at night as well."

Charles Palfour tugged at Hamish's sleeve. "Is the party still on?"

"If you mean the funeral, yes, I should think so."

"Come on, Olivia," called Charles. The pair ran off.

"Don't go falling in love with Mary Leinster," cautioned Elspeth.

"I haff no intention of doing such a thing. Mind your own business. Come along, Dick."

Dick winked at Elspeth and then trotted after Hamish.

Hamish appeared in the kitchen that evening with his fiery hair brushed and his tall, thin figure wearing his one best suit. Dick was extracting two clean cups from the dishwasher.

"You're supposed to wait until the machine is full," complained Hamish.

"Och, I'm just playing with it for a wee bit. I should go with ye."

"Why on earth?"

"Mary Leinster is a married woman."

"May I remind you this is the twenty-first century?"

"Oh, aye? Well, set your watch back two hundred years. This is Lochdubh. There'll be a right bit o' gossip in the morn."

"There's always a lot o' gossip. Lugs and Sonsie have been fed so don't feed them again."

"She like one o' thae china dolls," said Dick meditatively.

"Who?"

"Mary. You feel if you tilted her up, her eyes would close and if you pressed her belly button, she would say 'Mama.' "

"Stop havering. I'm off."

Mary was wearing a simple black sheath of a dress with a row of pearls. She smiled as Hamish joined her, and he felt a bit shy and uneasy.

Willie Lamont, the waiter who had once worked as a policeman, came bustling up. "The advocates with shrimp are good," he said, "and the veal misery is the special."

"He means the avocados with shrimp and the veal Marsala," translated Hamish.

She gave a little shudder. "I don't eat veal."

Willie leaned a confidential elbow on the table between them and said in a low voice, "It isnae really the veal, see, it's the pork fillet in disguise."

"Willie, go away and let us look at the menus in peace."

"Where's your husband the night?" Willie asked Mary.

Hamish stood up and marched Willie off into the kitchen and pushed him up against the wall. "You will quietly serve the meal or I'll push your teeth down your throat." He gave him a shake and went back to join Mary.

"Never mind him," said Hamish. "He's a bit eccentric."

When a chastened Willie reappeared, Mary ordered a feta salad and lasagne. Hamish ordered the same and a bottle of Valpolicello.

"You wanted to tell me something?" ventured Hamish at last, as Mary seemed to have relapsed into silence.

"You seem so sympathetic," said Mary. "I feel overburdened with trouble. People will be frightened to come to the glen now."

"Mary, I am sure today's publicity stunt will pay off. You'll have more tourists than ever."

"I resent you saying it was a publicity stunt."

"Oh, come on, Mary. That long-legged loon dancing around a barbecue and chanting in tongues?"

"I didn't think he'd turn out to be so weird," said Mary defiantly.

"And thon barbecue was hardly a consecrated altar. They were frying sausages on it as soon as the birds' ashes had been taken away."

She half rose from her seat. "If you are going to mock me . . ."

"No, no, lassie. My apologies. I can see you're sair troubled, and it's not just this business o' the glen."

Willie put their starter down in front of them. "Feckit," he said proudly.

"What did you just say?" demanded Hamish furiously.

"It's the feckit cheese. A big Irish man was in here last night and that's what he called it."

"It's feta cheese. Go away, Willie. Now, Mary," Hamish went on gently. "Out with it."

"Our marriage has just broken down in

bits," said Mary. "He hates the glen. He says I ought to be at home and start having children. I can't stand any more of it, Hamish." She reached across the table and took his hand.

Aware of the curious eyes of the other diners, Hamish gently removed his hand. "But you got him the contract to build the gift shop."

"Yes, but all that did was seem to make him think he should be in charge of everything."

"Mary, there's nothing I can do about it. He doesn't beat you, does he?"

"N-no."

"Then you need a divorce lawyer."

"Think of the scandal," said Mary helplessly. "People associate the glen with calmness and goodness. I've had the magic stepping-stones put in above the falls and little fairy footprints in the clay near the river."

Hamish felt he was being torn between cold logic and enchantment. The logic told him that he was dealing with a shrewd businesswoman who knew exactly what she was doing, but as he looked at her dainty, curvaceous figure and huge blue eyes, he felt he wanted her as he had never wanted any woman before.

Fern Palfour called down to her mother from the landing. Mrs. Colchester was sitting in an upright armchair in the shadowy hall. "Aren't you coming up to bed, Mother?"

"No, I'll sit here for a bit. There's something I have to work out."

"See you in the morning," said Fern. "Don't sit there too long. The evenings are getting cold."

Mrs. Colchester sat on in the deepening shadows of the hall. It was at the time of year when the nights never get really dark, and there was a faint eerie blue light shining down from the glass cupola overhead.

At last, she grasped her stick, hobbled over to the stair lift, and strapped herself in. Something made her look down. A gloved hand with a lighted match was stretching towards something under her chair.

The something under her chair was a powerful rocket. "Go away you horrible children," she shouted. "Just wait until I tell your father you've been playing with matches."

She pressed the button to start the chair. It hurtled upwards with a great whoosh. She struggled with the seat belt but it had been glued into place.

Mrs. Colchester shot upwards — the chair lift wrenched from its moorings by the force of the rocket — headed straight through the glass cupola at the top. For one brief moment, she seemed to hang in midair, silhouetted against the moon, and then she crashed straight down onto the stone terrace where her body lay in a mass of shattered chair.

Rivulets of blood seeped out from her broken body across the flagstones.

Hamish was just thinking that *comely* was the very word to describe Mary Leinster. Her soft arms were rounded and dimpled at the elbow. Her thick strawberry-blonde hair was as fine as a baby's and with a natural curl. And those eyes!

His phone rang shrilly. He was just about to answer it when Dick erupted into the restaurant. "Come quick!" he gasped. "The auld woman's dead. It's murder!"

Hamish called to Willie to put the price of the meal on his tab, made his excuses to a white-faced Mary, ran to the police station where he undressed and then scrambled into his uniform before heading off with Dick, the siren on the Land Rover setting the curtains of Lochdubh twitching aside.

When he arrived on the scene, Blair and Jimmy, Daviot, and SOCO were all there in force. His eyes travelled from the shattered body on the smashed chair and then up to the broken cupola on the roof.

Daviot was barking to various police officers to keep the gates to the lodge closed and keep any press at bay.

"Sir," said Hamish, "why couldn't she get her seat belt undone? That way she could ha' tumbled out of the chair before it hit the roof."

Daviot called to the head of the SOCO team. "Had a look at that seat belt?" he demanded.

"We think it's been superglued," said the white-coated figure. "Whatever bastard did this thought of everything."

Detective Chief Inspector Blair had seen Hamish talking to Daviot and lumbered forward. "You! Macbeth," he snapped. "Get down into that glen and see if there's anyone lurking around."

"You don't think it's got anything to do with anyone in the house?" asked Hamish.

"Don't you dare argue wi' me, laddie. You've got your orders."

"Come on, Dick," said Hamish. "Let's get

down to the glen before the press arrive."

"Waste o' time if you ask me," grumbled Dick.

They made their way through the car park and past the half-finished gift shop. Hamish stepped easily over the turnstile, which was locked, but had to help Dick over.

Hamish went down to the pool. The night was completely still, broken only by the sound of the waterfall. A reflection of the moon swam in the pool. Hamish unhitched a torch from his belt and shone it on the ground. "Someone's been down here recently," he said. "There are marks of footprints on the wet earth over by those rocks. You'd better hurry back and get someone down here to make casts of the prints. I'll go farther into the glen and see if I can see anything."

Hamish climbed up onto the bridge and followed the path on the other side. The glen had been planted at one time with a variety of deciduous trees, which were able to shelter there from the winds of Sutherland. A stand of silver birch stood out sharply against the moonlight, and the berries of the rowan trees looked as black as blood.

He stopped occasionally and stood, listening. There were various small tracks leading

85

away from the main path amongst the trees, but he felt impatiently that he was wasting time.

When he returned to the pool, two lab technicians were taking casts of the footprints. He went on up to the house in time to see Fern Palfour weeping as her husband was being escorted to a police car.

"What's happening?" Hamish asked Dick.

"Blair decided the son-in-law is guilty. Seems as though he was on the verge o' bankruptcy."

Hamish left him and went to join Jimmy Anderson. "What's the verdict so far?"

"It seems as if a rocket was put under that chair of hers and the seat belt superglued. At the landing before her bedroom, the banister had been sawn through so there was nothing to stop the impetus."

"How on earth could all these arrangements have been going on with people in the house?" marvelled Hamish.

"The rocket fuel was in a black canister right under the chair. Could have been put there anytime."

"Why drag Palfour off for questioning?"

"Because traces of potassium nitrate were found and he works in a nursery."

"It couldn't be the children, could it?" asked Hamish.

"Bit sophisticated even for them. I mean it wasn't any ordinary rocket. Took one hell of a thrust to send the old dear flying like that. Well, the mills of forensics grind slow but they grind exceedingly small. Blair's been too precipitate as usual. My bet is that Palfour will be back before dawn."

"Has Mrs. Palfour or the children been interviewed yet?"

"Need to wait until tomorrow. They've all been sedated."

"I'd like to get a look at the starting-off point," said Hamish.

"Don't see why not. Get suited up and I'll show you."

Hamish examined the place where the chair lift had started its murderous journey, noticing the long scorch mark on the bottom stair. He climbed up to where the banister had been sawn off and studied it. He called to Jimmy, who was following him up. "Come and have a look at this. Right, it was sawn through, but there are traces of glue. I think it was done when the house was quiet and then superglued together again. When everything was ready, all anyone would need to do was to pour a bottle of nail varnish remover over the banister, and it would be guaranteed to collapse under the force."

He climbed high until he was standing up under the glass cupola. "Now, why did that smash?" he said.

"That maid, Bertha, has been rousted out of bed. She said the glass was aye leaking water when it rained and Mrs. Colchester was too mean to get it repaired. She was carrying a stick. Maybe she pointed it at the glass in a last-ditch attempt to rescue herself and the whole thing shattered. Well, you saw the bloody mess that was left of her."

"I wonder who gets her money?" said Hamish. "Surely it stands to reason her daughter gets it."

"Not necessarily, if the maid's gossip was anything to go by. She didn't seem to like her daughter and she loathed her grandchildren. She was an odd old bird. The front door was never locked. Anyone could have walked in. The only place locked in here is the strong room where she kept her husband's collection of gold, silver, and jewellery."

"Is it all still there?"

"We won't know until the morning. The bank manager has the key and the key is in the bank vault, which is on a timer. She left a copy of her will with him as well." Jimmy stifled a yawn. "Better get some sleep while we can."

■ ■ ■ ■

Before he went to sleep, Hamish looked up how to make rocket fuel on the Internet. There were even videos showing you how to cook it up in your kitchen out of a mixture of cornstarch, potassium nitrate, corn syrup, sugar, and water. But surely that concoction alone would not have been as powerful as the one that sent old Mrs. Colchester sky-high.

Then maybe out on the moors there was some sort of test site. He drifted off into sleep and dreamt that he was looking down into the pool in the glen, and there, looking up at him from underneath the water and smiling, was Mary Leinster. He awoke with a jerk. He must put all thoughts of the woman out of his head. She had been just about to give more reasons for her divorce when Dick had burst into the restaurant with the news of the murder. But those blue eyes of hers were enough to addle any man's wits. It was rare to see such blue. People often had grey-blue eyes, or pale blue, but hardly ever that colour of the summer sky or like the blue of the kingfisher's wing.

Hamish's thoughts darkened. There was a psychotic killer on the loose. He was sure that the killing of the kingfishers was tied up with the death of Mrs. Colchester. To actually hang that poor bird from the branch was wicked. He did not like the Palfour children. They did not have the easy cheerfulness of children, and yet their parents seemed normal enough. Maybe it was the sort of free-for-all school they attended. He thought such schools had died out. Children without discipline could easily turn to crime. Then if the parents had enough money, they sent them to fashionable psychiatrists, always dumping the emotional burden on someone else. His final thought was that he was sure when he returned to the Colchester home in the morning, he would find Ralph Palfour, released from custody. Blair had acted like a bull in a china shop as usual. The police really had nothing to hold him on.

When he returned to the hunting box in the morning, it was to find Jimmy Anderson already there with his squad of detectives and police. Policewoman Annie Williams was playing on the front lawn with the children. She would rather have avoided the little horrors, but duty was duty and she had been ordered to keep them occupied. How could the children seem so carefree, wondered Hamish. Maybe all the violent shows on television and violent computer games had deadened their souls.

He approached Jimmy. "Where's Blair?"

"In bed. His wife, Mary, says he took a tumble down the stairs last night. Wouldn't blame her if she pushed him. The bank manager should be here soon and some lawyer from Strathbane."

"The motive can't be robbery," said Hamish, "if the key to the strong room was kept in the bank vault. Did you look for another one?"

"Maybe later. The forensic boys are still going over everything. Ralph Palfour is back."

Hamish grinned. "I thought he might be. Where's this nursery of his?"

"It's called Palfour Garden Centre and it's out in Fulham in London."

"Heffens! Think of the price of real estate. He could sell it to a developer for a fortune."

"I'll try him later on that. I gather the family has owned a garden centre there forever. Maybe there was something in his father's will forbidding him to sell it."

"I've been thinking, Jimmy, someone would want to test yon rocket. I'll bet somewhere up on the moors there's a test site."

"Good point. Why don't you take fat Dick there and go and search?"

"Will do. But come on, Jimmy, let me see what's in that strong room first."

"Right you are. Here they come."

Jimmy, Hamish, and Dick were standing outside the front entrance as two cars crunched their way over the gravel and came to a stop.

"Why a key?" demanded Hamish suddenly.

"What? Why?"

"I mean a strong room these days would surely have some sort of computerised entrance."

"It came wi' the house. Old Lord Growther's father had it installed. He went a bit weird in his old age and kept food in it."

"Food!"

"He thought his servants were stealing the food, so he locked it all up in there." He turned from Hamish to greet the new arrivals. "I am Detective Inspector Anderson," he said to the first man. "And you are?"

"I am Mr. Braintree from the bank."

"And I," said a man behind him, "am Mr. Strowthere, of Strowthere, Comlyx, and Frind, Mrs. Colchester's lawyers."

"Right," said Jimmy. "Follow me. We'll go

into the house from the terrace at the back. The forensic people are still going over the place. The strong room is just inside to the left at the end of a corridor."

They found Ralph and Fern Palfour waiting nervously for them on the terrace. They were introduced to the banker and lawyer. "May I know what was in my mother's will?" asked Fern.

"Good idea," said Jimmy. They all arranged themselves around a table on the terrace. Mr. Strowthere opened his briefcase. "Give us a simple summary," ordered Jimmy, "and you can go through the details later."

Mr. Strowthere cleared his throat. He's enjoying this, thought Hamish sourly. Pompous idiot. The lawyer was a plump florid man. "Mrs. Colchester," he began, "called on us a month ago and caused us to draw up a new will. In it, she leaves her money to Mary Leinster for the beautification of the Fairy Glen, formerly known as Buchan's Wood."

"She can't do that!" screamed Fern. "Is there nothing for me and the children?"

"Mr. Colchester has left this house and grounds to you, Mrs. Palfour, and all the plenishings of same house."

Odd Scots word *plenishings*, thought

Hamish. Means the contents. Still, I suppose if you can replenish, you can plenish.

Ralph clutched his wife's hand. "It's not that bad. There's supposed to be a fortune in the strong room."

"You mean she never showed you the contents?" asked Jimmy.

"Just the once," said Fern. "She said it was father's precious collection and it would come to me when she was dead."

Jimmy rose to his feet. "I think we should examine that strong room right away and discuss the contents of the will later."

Mr. Braintree led the small party into the house from the terrace and along a stone-flagged corridor to a massive iron door at the end. He was as thin as the lawyer was plump. His bones almost visibly creaked as he put a case on the floor and, after fumbling around inside, produced an enormous key.

He inserted it in the lock, twisted it, and the door swung open. He switched on a light. There were shelves stacked high with gold and silver ornaments: watches, epergnes, statues, clocks, snuff boxes, and various other precious objects. Glass cases held what seemed to be rare old maps. Fern Palfour had enough in here to kill for, thought Hamish.

The banker had taken out a thick inventory. "I will need to make sure everything is here," he said. On a table in the middle of the room was a large leather case. He approached it. "I will start by checking Mr. Colchester's jewellery."

"We'll leave you to it," said Jimmy, turning away, but Mr. Braintree had flung back the lid and let out a horrified gasp. Jimmy swung back. "What's up?"

"All the jewellery has gone," cried Mr. Braintree. "I checked the inventory two months ago and it was all here." He waved the inventory in the air in his distress.

"Give me a rough idea of what's missing," ordered Jimmy.

"A necklace of rubies and diamonds said to have belonged to the Empress Josephine, a diamond tiara and necklace, rings, bracelets, all precious, all worth millions. And at least four Fabergé eggs."

"There must be another key to this room," said Hamish. "Did Mrs. Colchester say she had another key?"

"No, never!" he gasped. "She was quite clear on that point. When she lodged the key with us, she said it was the only one."

"Where did she live before coming up here?" Jimmy asked Ralph.

"In London until just before Christmas.

She lived in a big house in Eaton Square. She was originally from the Hebrides and she said she missed Scotland."

"I'll need to get on to the Yard," said Jimmy. "Do you know the name of her bank in London?"

"Yes, it is the Grosvenor Merchant Bank. Her money and shares and so on are still there. She put only a small amount with us along with the key to the strong room."

"Who drew up the previous will?" asked Jimmy.

"We did," said the lawyer. "She said it was her first will. In it, she left everything to her daughter."

"I want that will contested," said Fern furiously. "Mary Leinster got to her some way."

"I don't see that Mary Leinster can gain personally from the money," said Hamish. "It will go to the trust, is that not the case, Mr. Braintree?"

"Yes, that is so."

"We'll leave you to the inventory," said Jimmy. "Mr. and Mrs. Palfour, if you don't mind, I wish to take statements from both of you."

He turned to Hamish. "I like that idea of a test site. See what you can find."

CHAPTER FIVE

The cruellest lies are often told in silence.
— Robert Louis Stevenson

Hamish felt quite sulky as he drove off with Dick. "I would have liked to stay for those interviews," he complained at last. "I don't like being sidelined."

"Well, that's what you get for being the village bobby," said Dick cheerfully. "Where do you think of looking first?"

"Perhaps that old quarry outside Craskie. They'd want something with a bit o' height."

"They?"

"I'm sure that more than one person is involved."

"What about Mary Leinster and her brothers?"

"Why them?" demanded Hamish sharply.

"Well, her millions go to Mary."

"Not to Mary. To the trust."

97

"Books can be fiddled."

"Don't be daft, man. Jimmy and his detectives will have thought o' that one. Now shut up and let me concentrate."

They searched the quarry, but there weren't any signs of sinister activity. Hamish sighed. "There's another one, off the Drim Road."

"I'm hungry," complained Dick.

"You're always hungry," snapped Hamish. Dick had put him in a bad mood by talking about Mary. Was he letting his feelings for her cloud his brain? Well, he would need to go on as usual, suspecting everyone. It was another rare sunny summer day, with the air dry enough to keep the horrible biting Scottish midges at bay. The mountains had that comforting blue look about them. It was only when rain was about to arrive that every detail stood out sharply as if on a steel engraving.

They reached the quarry outside Drim. Hamish let Sonsie and Lugs out and then filled up their feeding bowls and water bowls.

Dick muttered something under his breath about Hamish caring more for his pets than one hungry policeman. Hamish had parked on the lip of the quarry. He began to make his way carefully down the side with Dick stumbling and cursing after him. The roads that trucks had once used to enter the quarry were now made impassable with a thick carpet of brambles and gorse.

"I've got something," called Hamish from the floor of the quarry. Dick came panting up to join him. "See, there's a sort of cradle here that might have held a rocket, and there are scorch marks on the ground. I'd better phone Jimmy and get forensics onto this."

"Now can we eat?" asked Dick plaintively.

"Aye, we'll go into Drim. I want to ask Jock Kennedy who runs the local shop whether any strangers have been seen around."

Jock said that one of the locals, Andy Colluch, had said he thought someone was blasting in the old quarry a week ago but when Andy went there the next day he couldn't see anything. They got directions to Andy Colluch's croft. Dick dug his heels in and demanded food first. Ailsa, Jock's wife, took pity on him and said they sold hot snacks and she could let them have a couple of mutton pies.

Hamish waited impatiently until Dick had gulped down the last of his pie and said sharply, "Let's go."

Dick wondered what had happened to the usually laidback Hamish. But Hamish was feeling driven. It was the sheer malice and wickedness of the death of Mrs. Colchester that was getting to him. She could have been strangled, poisoned, or hit on the head. Why go to this elaborate means of murder?

Andy Colluch, a wizened old crofter, volunteered the information that as he was driving back from Strathbane a week ago, he thought he saw lights over by the old quarry and heard an explosion. He had gone up the following day to check whether someone was opening up the old quarry but had not seen anything.

Hamish phoned Jimmy with what he had found out, and Jimmy had said he would send a team over as soon as they had finished with the house. "We've found out something else," said Jimmy. "From the bits of the wreckage, it looks as if the engine of the stair lift had been tampered with and a more powerful one put in."

"When could all this have been done with people in the house?" demanded Hamish, exasperated.

"You'll never believe this," said Jimmy. "The day before, two men with cards claiming to come from the chair lift company said they had come to give the thing an overhaul. It wasn't a day for either of the cleaning women. The Palfours had taken the children out for a run in the car. Mrs. Colchester went to her room. She came down the stairs later under her own steam, saying she was not sure whether the men had finished."

"Why didn't they tell you before?"

"Because they didn't know," said Jimmy, "and I didn't know until the shepherd, Gale McBride, who runs his sheep on the grass there saw the men leaving and asked them what they had been doing. Bad description. Baseball caps pulled down over the eyes, answered in grunts, drove a pickup but Gale didn't get the registration."

"But it may mean someone inside the house was working with them," said Hamish.

"How do you make that out?"

"The superglue on the safety belt. If it had been put on earlier, it would have dried hard. Someone had to creep out of the shadows and doctor it just as she was about to make the ascent."

"Worse than that, we seem to have the world's press camped out up here. The Fairy Glen is coining it."

"What!"

"Aye, naturally the press want a look at

the place and that Mrs. Timoty is right there at the turnstile to charge them, along with all the other ghouls, and along with every teenager from miles around who hopes to be discovered by a television camera and become an instant celebrity. We've told Mary Leinster to close the place down for a week. We can't work with all this circus. We're getting auditors to go through the glen's trust fund to look for anything odd, and when they get their millions, believe me, the audits will go on."

"Are the Palfours still going to contest the will?"

"They've got enough out of that strong room to set them up for life. I don't think they'll bother. But folks seem to have gone fairy mad. They're saying the fairies did it."

"Mrs. Colchester said the day afore she died that she had something to tell me," said Hamish. "Maybe someone wanted her stopped."

"Could be."

"What does Annie Williams make of the children?"

"She says they have been traumatised."

"That precious pair! They didn't give a rap for their grandmother and openly wished her dead."

"She feels it's something that happened to

them afore they came up here but our Annie was aye softhearted. Stay where you are until the forensic people arrive."

Dick and Hamish sat down on flat rocks in the quarry and waited in the sunshine. Sonsie and Lugs had disappeared somewhere. Hamish told Dick the latest news.

"Highly technical fairies," said Dick. "I didnae think folk would still believe in them."

"They don't talk about it but the superstition runs deep. They're supposed to be little men, mischievous and resentful. Some say that maybe one time there was a smaller race of beings driven into hiding in the rounded hills by a stronger race. They mostly wear green and live in green hollow hills. They dance by moonlight, leaving marks of circles on the surface. They often ride in invisible procession, and all a man can hear is the shrill ringing of their bridles. They do not, as far as I know, run around fixing up stair lifts."

"It all comes back to Mary Leinster," said Dick.

"What does?"

"Whichever way you look at it, she benefits. Even after all the search for the murderers has died down, people will still be pouring into that glen. I bet she's already putting it about that old Mrs. Colchester offended the fairies. Her husband and brothers are builders. The two wardens are builders. They could all have combined to kill the old woman."

Hamish thought of Mary's blue eyes and felt saddened. There was an awful logic in what Dick had just said. Then he wondered if Elspeth Grant had been sent back up to report on the latest.

When the forensic team at last arrived, Hamish whistled for his pets and he and Dick went back to Lochdubh. Dick headed straight for the deck chair in the front garden, and Hamish went into his office to go through his notes.

The phone rang. It was Jimmy again. "I'm taking Mary Leinster in for questioning."

"Why?" asked Hamish with a sinking heart.

"The day before Mrs. Colchester met her death, she told a Mrs. Vance who works in the environmental department that she, Mary, had just had an attack of the second sight and had seen Mrs. Colchester in the sky, flying up against the moon."

"If the woman was guilty, she'd hardly want to advertise a murder," said Hamish.

"Some of thae psychos can be very cunning. Anyway, I'm taking her in. Annie's going to call on you to talk about the children."

Hamish hung up and sat frowning.

Second sight, or Dlama Shealladh as it was called in the Gaelic, was always impossible to prove. There was a superstition that if you talked about any foresight, then you would lose the ability to see things in the future. And the people who did talk, about foreseeing the death of someone for example, always talked about it *after* the event.

He heard Dick's voice from the garden. "Go round to the side door, Annie."

He went through to the kitchen to meet her. "I gather you've come to talk to me about the children," he said.

"Yes, they've been bothering me. They're not normal."

"Come in. Sit down. Do you want tea or coffee or something stronger?"

"I could murder a whisky."

Hamish took a bottle down from the cupboard and poured her a measure.

"So, sit down, lass, and tell me what's troubling you."

"I was worried about them before the murder." Annie sighed, taking off her cap and leaving it on a chair beside her. "My, but it's hot. There's something wrong there. It's as if something really nasty happened to them. They're closed in. They rely on each other because they dislike and distrust the whole human race. I wanted them to see a shrink but their parents turned that down flat. After they leave, there's not much I can do. Maybe there was abuse of some sort at that school they go to."

"They seemed anxious enough to get back to it, up to the point of wishing Granny dead," Hamish pointed out.

"Maybe you could have a try, Hamish."

"I won't be allowed to speak to them without the parents around."

"They didn't bother about me because they thought I was just playing with them to keep their spirits up."

"You mean try the same thing?"

"The parents have gone off to Strathbane to the lawyer's today. Mrs. Dunglass and Mrs. McColl, the cleaners, have said they'd keep an eye on them."

"Let's go, then," said Hamish. "I'll see what I can do."

He left Dick asleep in his chair in the garden and set off for Braikie with Annie following in her car. The weather was still fine but there was a dampness in the air. He glanced up at the sky. Mare's tails were spreading their long fingers in from the west, harbingers of a change in the weather. There was not a ripple to disturb the mirror surface of Lochdubh. People were standing in groups talking. It was all so peaceful. He had a sudden longing to turn round, go back and join Dick in the garden, and forget about the whole thing.

But instead, he accelerated out of Lochdubh and up over the moors and hills to Braikie.

Two policemen on duty opened the gates to the hunting lodge for them as they eased past the assembled members of the press. Not quite so many, he thought. The rest must be down at Strathbane.

Bertha Dunglass answered the door to them and said the children were in the garden.

They walked round the side of the building to the back. Olivia and Charles were sitting side by side, staring into space.

Hamish went over with Annie and sat on the grass next to them. There was a long silence. Then Hamish decided to take a gamble. "Tell me," he said softly, "why were you so anxious to go back to a school where you were both so badly treated?"

They looked at him, shocked expressions

on their faces. "How did you find out?" asked Charles in a choked voice.

"Well, Annie here, she thinks something bad happened to you afore you came up here and it has nothing to do with the murder. What is the name of your school?"

"Billhead Hall, in Barnet," said Olivia, her voice barely above a whisper.

"And it's sort of progressive, which means not much discipline. Now, in my experience," said Hamish in his soft lilting highland voice, "that can lead to lack of supervision, and that leads to bullying and all kinds of nastiness. Now, Olivia, answer me and remember I'll believe every word you say. Were you raped?"

"Charles stopped it in time," she said, her face whiter than ever.

"Go on."

"It's the art teacher, Mr. Smithers. He was always asking me to wait after class and stroking my hair. I got nervous. Charles hid in a cupboard in the art room. Smithers had me against the desk and was forcing me back, he had a hand up my skirt. Charles jumped out of the cupboard and struck him in the head with a vase. The police were called in. No one would believe us. I had a nasty medical examination. Nothing was found. Mr. Smithers said he wouldn't charge us. We were sent for sessions with the school shrink who told us that children of our age had vivid imaginations. It was like a nightmare. Even our own parents didn't believe us."

"When did all this take place?" asked Hamish.

"Near the end of last term."

"So why were you so reluctant to go to a comprehensive? You'd have been away from that awful school."

Charles said in a flat voice, "We were going back to kill him."

"I didn't hear that," said Hamish quickly. "If that gets out, they'll start thinking you murdered Granny. Why didn't your parents listen to you?"

"Mum's snobbish," said Olivia. "A lot of titled people send their kids there. They board them and then forget about them."

"What is Smithers's first name?"

"Jeffrey."

"With a *J?*"

"Right."

"Do you have a photograph of him?"

"Yes," said Charles. "There's one in the school brochure."

"And do you have it with you?"

"It's in my room. I'll get it."

They waited until he came back. Hamish

said, "Now, I'm going to tell you this," said Hamish. "I believe you and I'm going to fix this. When are your parents due back?"

"They said they would not be back until this evening. They want to avoid the press," said Olivia. Hamish felt a sudden surge of hatred for such parents who could leave their children alone when they needed support the most.

"I want you to sit tight. I will fix this for you and that includes Smithers."

They looked at him with a gleam of hope in their usually flat eyes.

"Annie, I want you to take them out of here, down to a movie in Strathbane, anywhere to cheer them up. Leave all this to me."

Elspeth Grant had come back north to cover the story. Hamish sped back to Lochdubh, where he phoned her. "Get over here to Lochdubh," he said. "I might be having the big story for you."

Elspeth walked into the police station to find Hamish in front of his computer, a school brochure spread out in front of him. He rapidly filled her in on the story. "I'm trawling through the pictures of sex offenders. Maybe that art teacher changed his name."

"You're putting yourself at risk, Hamish," said Elspeth anxiously. He swung round and found her silvery Gypsy eyes surveying him.

"Why?"

"Just a feeling."

"Oh, you and your feelings. Let me get on with this."

Elspeth pulled up a chair next to his. "There!" she said suddenly.

"How can you tell? He's got a beard. Smithers is clean-shaven."

"Use your imagination, Hamish. The eyes are the same. See how the left eye droops at the corner. Real name, Frederick Styles, charged with the rape of a nine-year-old girl ten years ago. Got eight years and out in six."

"Right. I'll report to Jimmy and get the wheels in motion. Those precious parents went down to Strathbane to see the lawyer. You might catch them there. If not, look for the most expensive restaurant in town. Don't tell anyone I tipped you off."

As Elspeth shot out of the police station, she nearly bumped into Dick, who was wiping the sleep from his eyes. Dick strolled into the station. "Don't suppose anything's been happening," he said. "Anything to eat?"

Elspeth was in luck. Ralph and Fern Pal-four were just emerging from the lawyers' offices when Elspeth approached them, microphone at the ready, filming already begun.

"We have just discovered," said Elspeth, "that your daughter was sexually attacked by her art master, a registered sex offender, and was only saved from rape by her brother. The man's real name is Frederick Styles. Why did you do nothing to protect your children?"

Fern burst into tears. Ralph tried to punch the cameraman who stepped nimbly out of the reach of his fist. "I'll sue you for this!" he howled.

"Please do," said Elspeth. "In the meantime, have you considered removing your children from that school?"

But Ralph and Fern had got into their car and roared off.

Hamish was later to wonder if all the resultant fuss had slowed down the investigation into Mrs. Colchester's death. Frederick Styles had disappeared and the police were searching for him. The Palfours were at one point in danger of having their children taken away from them. But a psychiatrist recommended that they should attend the local school in Braikie and try to lead normal lives while receiving counselling from him every week. Ralph and Fern Palfour were told that they were to stay in the Highlands until the police gave them permission to leave.

Mary Leinster had not been arrested. She insisted she had the second sight and that was that. On the evening of the murder, she said she had been at home with her husband.

Elspeth called on Hamish before heading south to thank him for the story. "It seems the sort of awful school where parents board difficult children just to get them out of the way. When I finally got to speak to Fern Palfour, all she would say was, 'But Lady Firthing sends her children there!' "

"I'm still puzzled by the violence and intricacy of the murder," said Hamish.

"Have you thought that it might have been done that way as a warning?"

"What do you mean?"

"I've a feeling," said Elspeth, "that someone out there knows something and has to be frightened into silence. And what makes it worse, someone *enjoyed* planning this murder. And what about Mary Leinster?"

"What about her?" demanded Hamish sharply. "There's no proof against her."

"If she didn't commit the murder," said Elspeth, "and I can't see her having the expertise, then she may be at risk. Either you believe in the second sight, either Mary was just showing off by saying she had a foresight of the murder, or she knows something and the murderer or murderers might consider she's a risk."

"You often have flashes of something verra like the second sight," said Hamish.

"I don't think it's that," said Elspeth slowly. "I think my brain gathers up all the knowledge and then gives me a feeling of something about to happen. Have you visited our famous seer?"

"Angus Macdonald. No. Why?"

"I'll bet Mary's been to see him at some point. He might be worth a visit."

Dick came into the kitchen carrying a shopping bag. "I've got some nice lamb chops here," he said. "Is it just you and me for supper or will Miss Grant be joining us?"

"Not me," said Elspeth. "I've got to be going. Be careful, Hamish."

"That's a grand lass," said Dick when

114

Elspeth had left. "I'll just be popping these chops on the stove."

"Give me about another hour, Dick. I've got someone to see."

Hamish found a box of cigars he had bought on a trip to Spain in his bedside drawer, and with the box tucked under his arm he went off to see Angus. The seer always expected a present. Hamish did not believe for a moment that the seer had any magical powers. He thought Angus relied on his wits and gossip.

A light drizzle was falling as he walked up the brae to Angus's cottage. The seer, shaggily bearded and wearing a ratty dressing gown, answered the door. He accepted the cigars and tucked them into his dressing gown pocket.

When they were seated in front of the smoking peat fire in Angus's living room, Hamish asked, "Have you had a visit from Mary Leinster?"

"Aye?"

"What did she want?"

Angus grinned, showing yellow nicotine-stained teeth. "Herself wanted to build me a grotto in the Fairy Glen. I was to sit there and say wise things to the tourists. I told her my arthritis wouldn't hear of it."

"Would you say she had the second sight?"

"I would say that one could see round corners. Cunning, she is."

"Come on, Angus. She's a pleasant woman who's bringing a lot of trade into Braikie."

"Set her cap at ye, has she?"

Hamish blushed. "Nothing like that."

"Aye, well, chust so long as she doesn't give you that auld chestnut about an unhappy marriage and so there's hope for one red-haired copper getting that cuddly body into bed."

"Whateffer gave you such a nasty idea?" said Hamish stiffly.

"You aye let the good ones get away, that's why."

Hamish's highland accent was pronounced. "I do not know what you are talking about. Chust mind your ain business in future."

"You came up here to make it my business," said Angus.

"I'm off!" Hamish headed for the door.

"Look out for the fairies," cackled Angus as Hamish slammed the door and set off down the brae.

He was taken aback to find Mary Leinster waiting for him in the kitchen, being served tea by Dick.

"Oh, Hamish!" she cried, when she saw him. Tears rolled down her cheeks.

"What's the matter?" demanded Hamish sharply. "Not another murder?"

As Mary gulped and sobbed, Dick explained. "Some residents of Braikie say that the glen was left to the public of Braikie. Nothing was ever said about charging admission. They are threatening to take Mary to court."

Hamish hung his peaked cap on a hook behind the door and sat down next to Mary. "Does the late Lord Growther's will say anything about not charging anyone?"

Mary shook her head. "But some of the townspeople are beginning to say we're greedy."

"There is one way round it," said Hamish. "Bus tours and car parties of people from outside the area pay the usual fee. The townspeople do not pay. That should settle the matter."

Mary took out a lace-edged handkerchief and dabbed at her eyes. "How clever you are!" she exclaimed. But there was a flash of something in those large blue eyes, gone in a minute. Hamish was suddenly reminded of the kingfisher.

"So," said Mary, "that's settled. I'll tell

117

the council tomorrow and get a broadcast on the local radio. I owe you dinner, Sergeant Macbeth."

Hamish hesitated. She looked at him, those magnificent eyes soft with appeal. He reflected dizzily that it was not often one saw a *rounded,* attractive woman these days. The fashion was for skinny muscular figures and high cheekbones. Mary was wearing a thin blue cashmere dress and small sapphire earrings.

Why not, he thought, suddenly angry with Elspeth and the seer for putting nasty thoughts about her in his head. "Grand," he said.

"I'll just hae the lamb chops and give the beasties some," said Dick cheerfully.

But as Mary preceded Hamish to the kitchen door, she found the wild cat, Sonsie, blocking her way, eyes yellow with hate and fur raised. Mary gave a cry of fright and backed against Hamish.

"Get lost, Sonsie!" shouted Hamish. "Out!"

The cat turned and slid out through the large cat flap. "Sorry about that," said Hamish. "I swear that animal gets jealous."

Mary took his arm as they walked outside, and dimpled up at him. "I can understand that."

The cat had joined the dog, Lugs, by the waterfront wall. They both turned and stared at Hamish and Mary.

"What . . . what unusual animals," gasped Mary. "I mean, a wild cat! And a dog with blue eyes!"

"They're grand beasts," said Hamish defensively, "and they've both saved my life on some occasions."

"How exciting! You must tell me about it."

Priscilla Halburton-Smythe, Hamish's ex-fiancée, arrived at the Tommel Castle Hotel for a brief visit. Her parents owned the hotel. The manager, Mr. Johnson, welcomed her, and Priscilla asked him about the murder which had been in all the news-papers.

When he had finished giving her all the gossip, Priscilla asked, "Where is Hamish this evening?"

"He's in the Italian restaurant right at this moment being bewitched, bothered, and bewildered by Mary Leinster."

"Indeed! The Fairy Glen woman?"

"The same."

"But she's married, isn't she?"

"There's a rumour she's getting a divorce. She claims to have the second sight."

"Pooh, and double pooh."

The window of the manager's office overlooked the car park. "I think a couple of your friends are out there, waiting for a word."

Priscilla joined him at the window. Sonsie and Lugs were sitting next to her BMW.

"How very odd," said Priscilla. "What do you think they want?"

"Those beasts give me the creeps. If they were human, I'd say they want you to get down to that restaurant and stop whatever is going on."

"They're probably just hoping for a free handout from the kitchens."

As soon as she had driven off, Mr. Johnson phoned Dick at the police station. "She's on her way with the cat and dog," he said. "Clever of you to sneak them up here."

"How did you know Mary Leinster and Hamish were having dinner?" asked Dick.

"As soon as they left the police station together, the jungle drums started beating. I thought if Priscilla felt obliged to take his pets back to him, it might throw a spanner in the works. He shouldn't be cavorting around with a murder suspect and a married one at that."

■ ■ ■ ■

Hamish was thinking pretty much the same thing. The restaurant was offering a cheap Recession Special, and the place was crowded. He was aware of curious and accusing eyes on him and his partner.

Willie Lamont, the waiter, took some time to get round to take their order. He had just written it down when the door of the restaurant opened. Priscilla entered with the cat and dog. Sonsie jumped on Hamish's back, pressed her furry chin on his shoulder, and glared balefully at Mary.

"Get off!" said Hamish furiously. "Priscilla, why are you here? And why did you bring Sonsie and Lugs?"

"I found them in the hotel car park. I was worried something might have happened to you, and Mr. Johnson told me where you were." Willie was quickly drawing out another chair at the table for Priscilla. "Come along," he said to Sonsie and Lugs. "Osso buco tonight." The cat plopped down onto the floor and, followed by Lugs, disappeared into the kitchen.

Hamish made the introductions. The two women surveyed each other. Mary was angry. Priscilla with her height and cool fair beauty was making her feel diminished.

Willie came back and Priscilla gave her order. Hamish wanted to protest that she hadn't been invited, until he quickly realised that her presence was restoring an air of respectability to his meeting with Mary.

"Tell me all about it," urged Priscilla. And Hamish, remembering how useful Priscilla had been as a sort of Watson in the past, began to outline everything he knew while Mary's face began to register boredom.

When Hamish had finished, Priscilla turned her attention to Mary. "It's a horrible business. What do you plan to do with the money?"

"We have to finish building the gift shop," said Mary, becoming animated. "Then we will be able to take out full-colour advertisements in all the major magazines. A lot of the paths through the woods need to be gravelled. Then I thought a Fairy Fete would be a good idea with the local children dressed as pixies and little lights hung through the trees. Oh, all sorts of ideas."

"But the whole sorry business started with the death of the kingfisher and then the sabotage of the bridge," said Priscilla. "Aren't you frightened that someone is out to put a stop to the tourists coming to the glen?"

"We'll now maybe be able to take on more people to patrol the place at night. We can't expect the present ones to work twenty-four hours. Some of the townspeople said they would patrol the glen but they didn't turn up."

"Don't you think the murder of Mrs. Colchester is somehow tied in with this?"

Mary gave a tinkling little laugh. "I expected a nice meal with Hamish here," she said. "I didn't expect to be grilled."

The door of the restaurant opened and Dick strolled in. "I burnt the chops, sir," he said to Hamish. "Oh, there doesn't seem to be a free table."

"It's all right," said Willie, suddenly appearing. "It's a good thing it's the big round table. Hamish aye gets this table when he's having dinner with Priscilla. Sit yourself down."

"Can't we talk about anything other than this dreadful murder?" said Mary, smiling up at Hamish. She put a hand on his. He gently drew his own hand away.

"It is verra hard to think o' anything else in the middle of a murder enquiry," said Hamish.

"And here's little me thinking it was my charms that lured you out for dinner," said Mary.

"Where is your husband this evening?" asked Priscilla sweetly. "As there are now so many of us, why don't you ask him to join us?"

Tears rolled down Mary's cheeks and she gave a pathetic little sob. "W-we don't get on. We're thinking of getting a divorce."

"With a possible divorce case coming up," said Priscilla, "it's better not to be seen in the company of any other man until the proceedings are over."

"I'm going to powder my nose," said Mary.

"You were a bit hard on her, Priscilla," said Hamish.

"I think she's making a fool of you."

"Well, you, more than anyone else, should know that that has happened to me before," said Hamish angrily. "Aren't you going to order anything to eat, Dick?"

"No, I'll just eat Mary's."

"What!"

"No point in wasting good food. She won't be back."

Willie came up to the table. "Thon Mrs. Leinster walked right through the kitchen and out the back door."

Hamish half rose to his feet and then sank back down into his chair. He began for the first time to feel that in some way Mary was trying to manipulate him, and if that were the case, then why?

"What about the Palfours?" asked Priscilla. "The children were abused at that school. What kind of parents just ignore that?"

"They were both boarded," said Hamish. "Husband and wife work in that nursery. They've got people running it for them at the moment. Parents sometimes send difficult children to schools like that just to get them out of the way."

"Meaning there might have been something wrong with the Palfour children before the abuse at the school?"

"The police psychiatrist is working with them. Maybe he'll come up with something. But a couple of kids wouldn't have the expertise to make that rocket and then soup up the engine."

"Maybe. What is Mary Leinster's background and how did she become such a power in Braikie?"

"She was working with the council in Perth. She has a degree in environmental studies. When Lord Growther left the glen to Braikie, they didn't do anything about it. But just before this new government, councils were going daft employing all sorts of people. They advertised for an environmental officer and Mary got the job. Her husband and brothers came up with her."

"Where she found them a contract to build the gift shop?"

"That was approved by the council."

"I wonder why. I wonder if Mary flirted or worse with the provost and members of the council and then applied a little genteel blackmail."

"Priscilla!" exclaimed Hamish. "I am not a fool!"

"I'll give Mary Leinster this," said Priscilla. "That one could fool any man."

Once back at the police station, Hamish rounded on Dick. "Those beasts didn't get up to the hotel under their own steam. You drove them there. How did you know Priscilla was back?"

"Mrs. Wellington, the minister's wife, told me but she said not to tell you because it would only upset you. I'm sorry if I overstepped the mark, sir, but Mary Leinster frightens me. There's something at the back of the eyes. Something like you see in the eyes of a bird o' prey, or o' a kingfisher spotting a nice fat trout. Where are you off to now?" he asked as Hamish headed for the door.

"I'm going up to have a look at that glen.

126

I want peace and quiet to see the place for myself."

CHAPTER SIX

From the loan shieling of the misty island
Mountains divide us, and the waste of
   seas —
Yet still the blood is strong, the heart is
   Highland,
And we in dreams behold the Hebrides!
               — Sir Walter Scott

The long twilight, or gloaming, of a highland summer's night when it never really gets dark surrounded Hamish as he sat down on a smooth rock by the pool. Everything was utterly silent, except for the rushing of the waterfall.

He realised he had to have this time to be really alone. He liked Dick, but Hamish was used to his own company. Of course, Elspeth would point out acidly that he was married to his cat and dog.

What on earth did he see in Mary Leinster? Perhaps it was because these days one did not come across such sheer femininity. Clothes, hair, perfume, and blue eyes, all supplied in an alluring package.

Quite suddenly he fell into a dreamless sleep, deep and black as velvet. He awoke with a start with the early sun in his eyes and took a deep breath of clean air.

The glen looked enchanting and enchanted. A thin veil of mist was rising above the pool, and little rainbows were dancing in the waterfall. He felt a surge of joy. It was like the beginning of the world before sin and evil. He could almost believe in such a place as the Garden of Eden before the snake.

With the dawn chorus in his ears, he climbed up to the car park, surprised that he wasn't feeling the least bit stiff.

He was about get into his Land Rover when he remembered that Mrs. Colchester had been in the habit of visiting the pool alone at night. She had evidently stopped doing so before her murder.

The very grotesque way in which the murder had been committed, he was sure now, had been a warning: a mafia-type warning to anyone in the know to keep their mouths shut. Jimmy had left a report in the notes to say that the two men who had come to service the lift had not been traced.

He drove thoughtfully back to the police station. There was a message on his desk from Dick. "Mrs. Colchester is to be buried at her request on some island called Rosse. She evidently was born there. Body's been released. Funeral tomorrow. Daviot wants us to go along and see who turns up."

Rosse, thought Hamish. Does anyone live there? He pulled down a map of the Western Isles. There was Rosse, slightly to the south of Tiree, not much more than a dot on the map.

As he stared at the map, he began to wonder how long he could keep his police station. There were plans afoot to axe sixteen police stations in the north of Scotland, including the one at Nairn which had been built a year ago at a cost of just over one million pounds. He remembered a doctor saying to him cynically that if he ever wanted to know a hospital the government was about to close down, then look for the one that had just had a new ward built.

And what would happen to his own beloved station? Or would he be now expected to police the whole of the north of Scotland?

He roused Dick, made breakfast, and then phoned Jimmy and asked about the funeral arrangements. "I've told the Palfours I am sending you along," said Jimmy. "They feel they need protection. No need to take Fraser with you. They're setting out tomorrow with the coffin. Ferry to Tiree and then fishing boat to Rosse. The Palfours had to pay a whack to get a fisherman who'd take a coffin on board, let alone a woman. Superstitious lot."

"Does anyone live there?" asked Hamish.

"Couple o' old crofters. Brothers. Ezekiel and Abraham McSporran. Now, there's a couple o' names to conjure with. They were both married one time but the wives died and there were no children. They're reputed to be a bit weird. You're to take camping equipment. The minister in Tiree is putting up the Palfours but he says there's no room for you. Mrs. Colchester's father and mother lived there for a short time before he went over to the mainland."

"When do we all set off?"

"Six o'clock tomorrow morning to catch the ferry from Oban."

"How's the rest of the investigation going?"

"For the rocket, anyone can buy potassium off the Internet and there's potassium in fertiliser. You would think the Leinsters would be prime suspects, but they didn't want their glen wrecked. The money the old woman left them goes into the trust, and the council auditors monitor it. Scotland Yard can't dig up anything out o' the London background."

"When did Mrs. Colchester arrive on the mainland?"

"About the time o' the ark. Her parents, Mr. and Mrs. Mackay, were crofters on Rosse but they found the life too harsh and moved to Strathbane. Father got a job in a slaughterhouse. Mrs. Colchester worked as a nurse in Strathbane and then moved to London. Worked at Guy's Hospital and nursed Colchester when he had an operation to remove his appendix. Married him and became a wealthy woman."

"And the parents?"

"They died soon after she was married. They weren't invited to the wedding and then she never even went to their funerals. Got a reputation as being really cruel and nasty."

"Maybe," said Hamish, "there's someone we don't know about. Maybe some other relative."

"Believe me, man, we've dug up the family tree by the roots and there isn't anyone."

"What age was Colchester when he married?"

"Thirty-eight?"

"And the nurse?"

"Twenty-two."

"And Colchester was a wealthy man. Hadn't he been married before?"

"No, but he was engaged to a Miss Crystal Hunter, a socialite. She's dead. Never mind, Hamish. Do your bit at the funeral."

A few people stood on their doorsteps in Braikie at dawn the following morning to watch the hearse bearing Mrs. Colchester's body go by. The Palfours followed in their car and, behind them, Hamish in the Land Rover.

As if in keeping with the solemnity of the occasion, a thin, greasy drizzle was falling as they boarded the car ferry at Oban. There is normally a beautiful view of the islands from Oban Bay, but on that morning everything was shrouded in a thin mist.

Hamish would have liked to pass the journey by talking to the Palfours, but Ralph told him sharply to leave them alone in their grief.

Glad that he had had the foresight to bring some paperbacks with him, Hamish settled down to read and pass the four-hour journey. The ferry ploughed on in the shelter of the Isle of Mull. Once past Ardnamurchan Point, the sun came out and Hamish left his book and went out to lean on the rail, looking up at the famous Ardnamurchan Lighthouse as the ferry pushed on towards the Island of Coll.

The ferry stopped at Arinagour on Coll and after unloading passengers and cargo headed out for another hour's journey to Gott Bay on Tiree.

The Island of Tiree has more sunshine than anywhere else on the British Isles because it is extremely flat, parts of it inland being under sea level, and any bad weather just races over it. Hamish remembered that at some places on the island, you would think the whole of the Atlantic Ocean was going to come pouring in on you.

A Church of Scotland minister, a Mr. McCluskey, was at the jetty to meet them. He was a tall, thin man with greying hair, a pleasant smile, and a lilting voice.

He shook hands with the Palfours and then said to Hamish, "Geordie, along there on the *Highland Queen,* will take you over to Rosse today to get settled and we will be over tomorrow for the funeral. It is an odd sort of arrangement. I suggested to your superior, Detective Chief Inspector Blair, that we could surely find you some accommodation on the island, but he said you were used to roughing it and they were economising on their police budget."

Hamish thanked him although he mentally cursed Blair. He unloaded his camping equipment from the Land Rover, and carrying his rolled-up tent under his arm, with the rest of his equipment packed into a heavy backpack, he set off for the *Highland Queen,* where he was hailed by the weather-beaten, grizzled skipper.

"I'm going to charge you lot a fair whack for this," said Geordie as his "crew" consisting of one sullen youth helped Hamish aboard. "It iss the rare bad luck to take a wumman aboard let alone a coffin and that iss what I'll be doing the morrow."

"I'll need to go into Scarinish first and get some food," said Hamish. "I don't suppose there's any on Rosse?"

"Sheep. That's all."

Hamish got off the boat and shopped quickly, trying not to buy too heavy a load. When he returned to the fishing boat, he stored his groceries in his backpack.

"What are the McSporrans like?" asked Hamish as the boat began to chug out of the harbour.

"I do not believe in the gossip," said Geordie. "It iss the devil's work."

Hamish contented himself by watching the blue and green water. A dolphin rose up beside the boat in a high arc and di‑

135

appeared beneath the waves.

The Island of Rosse soon appeared, at first looking nothing more than a rocky outcrop sticking up above the waves, but as they approached, Hamish began to make out a stone jetty and, behind it up on a grassy hillside, a white croft house, the grass surrounding it dotted with sheep.

Hamish had planned to tip the skipper, but once his goods were unloaded, the boat backed out and roared back in the direction of Tiree without Geordie having said one word.

He heaved his backpack onto his shoulders, set off up the hill for the nearest of the cottages, and knocked at the door.

A very small man opened the door to him, a troll-like figure. His nut-brown face was crisscrossed with wrinkles. His thick grey hair was wild and shaggy, and he had hair sprouting from his nostrils and his ears.

"Good day," said Hamish politely. "Can you suggest a good place where I can pitch my tent?"

Small flat grey eyes looked up at him. They stared at each other in silence. Hamish sighed and repeated his question in Gaelic.

The answer came in Gaelic. "Find out for yourself," and the door was slammed in his ce.

Hamish started off to see if he could find a stream with fresh water and at last located one on the far side of the small island. Puffins popped out of their burrows and stared at this newcomer. A herring gull flew past and eyed him malevolently.

No wonder Mrs. Colchester's parents wanted to get off this place, thought Hamish. What was her maiden name again? It was somewhere in his notes. Mackay, that was it. He had passed a couple of ruined cottages in his search. Maybe she had been brought up in one of them.

The stream ran down to a small sandy beach dotted with smooth black rocks. Two seals heaved themselves out of the water and climbed onto the rocks.

He erected his tent, lit his camping stove, and began to cook sausages and bacon on a frying pan. After that, he boiled up a billycan to make tea and began to feel more cheerful. Little waves lapped on the beach, and the sun was warm on his back.

After he had finished eating, he packed everything away in the tent, propped his back against a rock, and started to read. In no time at all, he was asleep.

He awoke an hour later and then sat up with a jerk. The calm blue sea had turned blackish grey, and a stiff gale was blowing.

He had placed his tent in the lee of one of the island's only small hills, but the wind was increasing as were the waves.

Cursing, he dismantled the tent, rolled it up, and repacked his backpack. He set off inland, staggering now before the force of the gale. Hamish reached the first of the ruined crofts, but there seemed to be no shelter even there, for the gale was now shrieking and tearing at him.

A small, male figure suddenly seemed to materialise in front of him. He jerked his head and Hamish followed him, from time to time almost being swept off his feet by the force of the gale. No rain fell although black clouds hurtled past overhead.

The man led the way to the croft house Hamish had first visited. Hamish followed him in. "We cannae be leaving you out in this weather," said his host. "I'm Ezekiel McSporran, and thon by the fire is my brither, Abraham."

Abraham, whom Hamish had spoken to earlier, looked like a troll-like copy of his brother. Hamish wondered if they were twins. He stacked his tent and backpack just inside the door and gratefully joined them in a seat in front of the fire.

"This is right kind of you," said Hamish, glad that they could speak English after all because his Gaelic was pretty rusty.

"You shouldnae be bringing her back here," said Abraham. "They don't like it."

"Who are they?" asked Hamish.

They both looked at him in silence.

The living room was stone-flagged with a box bed in a recess in one corner. He could see there was a small kitchen at the back. There didn't seem to be any other rooms in the tiny house. A small window revealed that the walls were very thick.

There were a few brass ornaments on the mantelpiece. Otherwise, the room was bare except for the three battered armchairs they were sitting on.

Hamish remembered he had a bottle of whisky in his backpack. He went and got it and presented it to Ezekiel.

"My, that's grand," said Ezekiel, showing the first signs of animation. Abraham went into the kitchen and came back with three glasses. Hamish then unpacked all the groceries he had left and followed him into the kitchen. He placed his offerings on the counter: half a packet of bacon, sausages, bread, milk, cheese, tea and sugar, two cans of beans, and a loaf of bread.

"I need to use the toilet," said Hamish.

"Out the back," said Abraham.

Hamish opened the back door and

plunged out into the storm. A hut lashed down with ropes was, he assumed, the lavatory. It smelled horribly inside but he realised he would have to use it.

When he returned to the house, the brothers had put a battered card table in front of the fire with three glasses on it. Abraham filled three small glasses with whisky.

"Slainte!" said Hamish.

They nodded and clinked their glasses against his own. Outside, the gale had risen to an eldritch shriek as if all the spirits of hell were riding the heavens.

"Why did Mr. Mackay leave?" asked Hamish.

"They frightened him off," said Ezekiel, after a long pause.

"Who?"

"We don't talk about them. It's bad luck," said Abraham.

I'm sure this daft pair think the fairies drove them away, thought Hamish, when any man can see you'd need to be mad to stay in a place like this.

"Where do you sell your sheep?" asked Hamish.

"Every year. The Lairg sheep sales," said Abraham.

"That's quite a bit o' organisation," said Hamish, thinking they would need to get their sheep to Tiree and then onto a lorry and then onto the ferry.

"We're used to it."

"Get a good price?"

"Aye, we do well," said Ezekiel. "It's rough here but the grass is rare fine."

"This funeral," said Hamish cautiously. "Where is it to be? I didn't see any church on the island."

Ezekiel said, "Me and Abraham dug a grave already out by the old Mackay croft. Some of the men from Tiree came over to help us. It wass hard going."

"Do you play cards?" asked Abraham, refilling the glasses.

"Not often," said Hamish. "What's your game?"

"Snap," said Ezekiel.

"Oh, I can play that," said Hamish, relieved to hear it was to be a children's game of cards and not something like bridge of which he knew nothing at all.

The brothers took the game seriously, roaring out a triumphant "Snap" when one got a matching card, hitting the table so hard in their enthusiasm that Hamish was afraid it might collapse.

At last, the whisky being finished, Abraham went into the kitchen to prepare dinner. Ezekiel had found a Bible and had started to read. Hamish got a detective story out of his backpack and read until dinner was served.

The meal was a simple one: boiled potatoes and oatmeal covered in shreds of seagull.

"That's baby cormorant," said Abraham proudly. "They got a rare taste."

"I didn't think you could get cormorants here," said Hamish. "No cliffs."

"Get them over on Vole Bay in Tiree."

After dinner, Ezekiel read aloud from the Bible, a long chapter from the Old Testament which seemed to be full of begats.

Then he held up a gnarled finger and said, "Listen!"

The night had become quiet. Ezekiel rose and opened the door. Hamish followed him. Outside the night was calm, clear, and starry.

"Grand thing, the Bible," said Ezekiel. "We're off to bed. You can put your bedroll by the fire."

The brothers undressed down to long grimy underwear and climbed, one after the other, into the recessed bed and drew the curtains.

Hamish was wearing the casual clothes he had changed into before the storm had risen. He took out his uniform and cap and laid them across one of the chairs.

Then he got into his sleeping bag and fell into a dreamless sleep, not waking until Abraham shook him in the morning.

As the fishing boat approached the jetty, it was a clear, calm day, as if the horrors of the storm had never happened. The coffin was put onto a hospital trolley and wheeled along the jetty. The Palfours, the minister, and Hamish followed the coffin and the brothers across the grassy island to one of the ruined crofts, where a deep grave had been dug.

The minister began the service. The Palfours stood holding hands, dry-eyed.

When it was finally over, Fern Palfour, who had been carrying a small plastic bag, extracted from it a spray of hawthorn blossom and threw it down on top of the coffin. "Mother said in her will there were to be no flowers, but the coffin looks so bare and . . ."

Ezekiel fell to his knees and began to pray. Abraham let out a screech of horror and jumped down into the grave. Hamish was frightened he would split the coffin. Abraham grabbed the hawthorn and crawled out with it. His face was contorted with fury.

"You stuppit bitch!" he howled at Fern.

"That's the fairy flower. You'll bring bad luck." Then he set off at a run across the island, holding the spray of hawthorn in his hand.

"What have I done?" asked Fern, bewildered. But even highland Hamish knew the answer to that one. "It's the fairy tree," he said. "You're not supposed to touch it. They don't like it."

Goodness, he thought, I'm beginning to sound as daft as the brothers.

Ezekiel had risen to his knees and was desperately shovelling earth down into the grave. Hamish saw another spade close by, stripped off his regulation jersey, and began to help him.

When the sorry little procession finally made its way down to the fishing boat, the minister said to Hamish, "This is a bad business."

"You surely don't believe in the fairies, sir," said Hamish.

"No, no. I was thinking of Mr. and Mrs. Palfour. Such an un-Christian exhibition."

"It seems there are some places in the world where people can believe in magic and religion at the same time," said Hamish. "Besides, I get the impression the daughter is not exactly mourning the death of her

144

mother."

"She is probably still in shock," said the minister severely. "Her mother met a dreadful end."

On the long journey back to Sutherland, the Palfours avoided Hamish, and any attempts he made to speak to them on the Oban ferry were met with stony silence.

It was only when he reached the police station and began to answer Dick's eager questions about the funeral that Hamish realised he was very tired. He told Dick he was going to bed and retired with the dog and cat following him.

He awoke the next morning to the throb of the dishwasher and the welcome smell of frying food.

He rose, washed, dressed, and went into the kitchen, where Dick was frying up breakfast.

"Sit down, sir, and get that down ye." Dick put a plate of fried sausages, bacon, fried haggis, black pudding, and two eggs in front of Hamish.

"You're getting to be a grand cook," said Hamish, realising he was ravenously hungry. "Any news?"

"Jimmy Anderson is going to call this morning."

"Then let's hope he has something for me," said Hamish.

"And that Mary Leinster came round. I reminded her you were at the funeral and she said she'd forgotten."

"Did she say what she wanted?"

"I think she just wants you."

"Havers, Dick. I don't mess around with married women."

"If you say so."

When breakfast was over and the dishwasher was finally silent, Dick opened it to take out the clean plates and put in the dirty ones. Hamish noticed to his irritation that Dick was taking out two mugs and one plate, two knives and forks, and a whisky glass.

He was just complaining, "Man, you're going to land me with a huge electricity bill if you don't stop playing with that thing," when Jimmy gave a perfunctory knock at the door then walked straight in.

"Get anything out of the Palfours?" he asked.

"Not a thing," said Hamish. He described his time on the island and the funeral.

"I think there's insanity behind all this," said Jimmy. "Some downright psycho. What about the Leinsters? Maybe the old girl had found a way out of them keeping the glen?

Maybe they killed her to get their hands on the money. I wish to God we could trace those two men who claimed they were servicing the stair lift."

"But I assume you'll be keeping a close eye on the trust's accounts."

"Aye, but we can't keep auditing them forever. And what happens then? A bit siphoned off here and there into their pockets."

"What about Mary Leinster's husband and brothers?" asked Hamish.

"That would be Tim Leinster and Brad and Angus Brooke. Aye, well, they were grilled by Blair shouting in their faces, Mary accused of nepotism in giving them the contract to build the gift shop, Blair suspended again as Mary threatened to sue. Daviot told us to back off for a bit, and it was a mess all round. There were no prints on that saw, but that in itself is suspicious."

"Mary's keen on our Hamish," said Dick cheerfully.

Jimmy's face looked even foxier than usual. "Is she now? You should make use of that, Hamish. Did she tell you she was unhappily married or something?"

"Well, she did," mumbled Hamish.

"We've got to solve this case, Hamish, so you get over to that town hall and cosy up to her. Is she really unhappily married or just stringing you along?"

"I'd like a word with her husband first," said Hamish mulishly.

"What? What are you going to ask him? Have you stopped beating your wife?"

"Nothing like that. I want to get an impression o' the man."

"All right. You'll find them building that gift shop but suss out Mary whatever it takes, and that's an order!"

The brothers were taking it easy, drinking tea over a camp stove, when Hamish approached them.

"What now?" demanded Angus. "We've been answering questions until we're fair black in the face. Our Mary's going to sue you lot for harassment."

Hamish surveyed them. It was hard to imagine they were Mary's brothers. Their hair was brown and their eyes, pale blue. They were both tall with strong, muscular figures.

"It won't take long," said Hamish soothingly. "I feel somehow that the death of the kingfisher, the wreck of the bridge, and the murder of Mrs. Colchester are somehow all tied up. Have either of you any ideas about the matter?"

"We've talked about it," said Angus. "There's only the one idea. On the council, there was only one man that was against the glen, Councillor Jarvis. He's the one that has the hardware shop in the main street in Braikie. He said we were making a circus out of the place but he was voted down. Now, we aren't saying he would murder the old woman, but I wouldn't put it past him to try to spoil the glen and drive people away."

"Is he a powerful enough man to have been able to saw through the bridge?"

"Well, he knows how to use a saw," said Angus.

"Now, I've one more delicate question to ask you. Is your sister happily married?"

"Aye," said Angus, looking surprised. "Someone's been gossiping?"

"Something like that," said Hamish. "I'll be having a word with this councillor."

The hardware shop had an old-fashioned front with JARVIS in gold letters over the entrance. Hamish pushed open the door and went in.

"Mr. Jarvis?"

"That's me," said the man behind the counter. He was wearing a brown overall over his clothes. He was tall and gangly with

149

grey hair and a large nose which dominated his face. His hands, which were resting on the counter, were large and powerful.

"I am Sergeant Hamish Macbeth from Lochdubh. I am investigating the sabotage to the glen."

"Wouldn't you be better off trying to find out who murdered the old woman?" he demanded truculently.

"One thing at a time," said Hamish. "I believe only you were opposed to turning the glen into a tourist attraction."

"It should be left as a quiet place for the locals," he said. "Not turned into some sort of Disney playground. But all that Mary Leinster had to do was seduce my colleagues into agreeing."

"You don't mean she actually, physically seduced any of them?"

"Wouldn't surprise me in the slightest. Before the vote, I saw her out to dinner with one or t'other, flirting like mad."

"That bridge was sawn in such a way to make sure it would collapse when a busload of tourists walked on it," said Hamish. "Can you think of anyone who might have wanted to do that?"

He gave a rather nasty laugh. "Meaning, did I do it? Forget it. Maybe it was the provost's wife."

"I can't see a woman having the strength or knowledge to do that," said Hamish.

"Then you haven't met Gloria McQueen."

"The provost's wife?"

"Aye, herself has been heard threatening to kill Mary."

"Maybe I'll be having a word with her. Has anyone bought a power saw from you in, say, the past month?"

"Wait a minute and I'll check the book."

The shop was stocked from floor to ceiling with all sorts of tools and implements. Three lawn mowers stood just inside the door. The shop was dark and shadowy although there were two unlit fluorescent tubes overhead.

Jarvis came back. "No. No one," he said to one of the lawn mowers by the door.

"Are you sure?" Hamish was suddenly convinced he was lying.

"Of course I am sure. I am not in the way of being called a liar."

"Where does Mrs. McQueen live?"

"A big villa up at the end of Barry's Close. You can't miss it."

Somehow glad to have an excuse to put off seeing Mary, Hamish drove up to Barry's Close in the "posh" part of town. He parked and went up to the tall wrought-iron gates which guarded the entrance to the villa. He pushed one open and walked up a short curving gravelled drive to the large Victorian villa, home to the provost.

He was just about to ring the bell when he heard the sound of a saw coming from the back of the house. He walked around the side of the building to the back.

A burly woman wearing a checked shirt and men's trousers with a headscarf over her grey hair was attacking a stand of silver birch at the corner of the back garden with a chain saw.

She saw Hamish approach and switched off the saw. Her large round face was red from exertion. "It's Macbeth, isn't it?" she demanded. "What do you want?"

Two birch trees had been felled, their silver trunks lying across the edge of the lawn.

"Why are you cutting down those beautiful trees?" demanded Hamish.

"It's none of your business what I do on my own property," she snapped. "What do you want?"

Hamish suddenly did not quite know how to begin. Well, he thought, may as well plunge right in.

"It's said you were heard threatening to kill Mary Leinster."

"What's that to do with anything? She's alive, isn't she? Besides, everyone says 'I could kill you' at some time or another, but they don't do it."

"The thing is," said Hamish patiently, "that someone tried to sabotage the glen, and I can see you're a dab hand at wielding a chain saw."

"I will be speaking to your superior," she said. "How dare you insult me. Get out!"

"I would nonetheless like to take a statement from you," said Hamish stubbornly.

"Don't be silly. Get lost. There are some things I could tell you but I can't be bothered." She started up the chain saw again and began to attack another tree.

Hamish decided he could not really put off seeing Mary any longer. He would need to get her side of the story. As he walked towards his Land Rover, he remembered that Dick had an amazing fund of gossip and phoned him.

He could hear the dishwasher whirring away in the background. "Have you heard anything about the provost's wife threatening to kill Mary?"

"Aye, the Currie sisters said something about that the other day."

"For heffen's sake, man, why didn't you tell me?"

"Och, you know the twins. Just malicious tittle-tattle most o' the time."

"Gie me patience," groaned Hamish. "What exactly did they say?"

"It was a week ago and the provost and Mary had lunch at the pub in Braikie. When they came out, there was Gloria McQueen, evidently a right battle-axe. She calls Mary a whore and accuses her of trying to get off with her old man. Says she'll kill her if she doesn't leave him alone. McQueen starts to bleat it was only a business lunch. Gloria says, 'Bollocks. I'll see you when you get home.' Next day the provost has a black eye."

"Dick! If she's beating him up, it's a police matter."

"Och, she probably just lost her rag the once," said Dick.

"See to it," said Hamish grimly. "Get over to Braikie and ask the provost about the incident."

"Oh, sir, I amn't that good wi' the high and mighty."

"Then it's time you learned," said Hamish, and rang off.

Mary was not in her office. He waited an hour outside until he saw her coming back. "I need to have a word with you," said

Hamish, avoiding those blue eyes.

"Good. I'm just off to have lunch in the pub. Join me?"

"It would be better and make it more official," said Hamish stolidly, "if I were to interview you in your office."

"And go hungry?" She put a hand on his arm and smiled up at him. "Come along, silly. Lunch is on me."

What was it about her? wondered Hamish as he allowed himself to be gently led to the pub across the road. She emanated a sort of force field of sensuality and femininity. She was wearing a white blouse and a short pleated tartan skirt. Her tights were sheer black, and her shoes of patent leather had very high heels.

Once seated in the pub, Mary gently insisted that they order their food before "business." She chose steak and chips and a bottle of Côtes du Rhône. Hamish asked for a club sandwich and remarked, "No wine for me. I'm driving."

"Now," she said, putting dimpled elbows on the table. "Fire away."

Hamish repeated what he had heard about the confrontation with Gloria McQueen.

"Oh, that," said Mary with a shrug. "Awful woman. She makes his life a hell. We were only discussing business."

"Do you know that she has, and can wield, a chain saw?"

"Really? Do you think she might have sabotaged the bridge?"

"It is possible. I've sent Dick to interview the provost. If she's in the habit of beating her husband, it's a police matter."

Mary gave a tinkling laugh. "Where's your proof?"

"He had a black eye the day after the confrontation."

"Oh, he'll probably say he walked into a door."

"Did he say anything to you?"

"Here's our food," said Mary. "Gosh, I'm hungry. Are you sure you won't even have just the one glass of wine?"

"No, I'll stick to water," said Hamish. "I repeat, did the provost say anything to you about his wife beating him?"

"No, it was just business."

She's lying, thought Hamish. Why do I find her so attractive when I don't trust her one inch?

"Well, well, well," said a fake hearty voice. Hamish looked up and then got to his feet. "Mr. McQueen," said Hamish. "We were just talking about you."

McQueen was a small round man, like Tweedledum. His face glistened with sweat.

Out of the corner of his eye, Hamish saw Mary give an infinitesimal shake of her head. She's telling him she hasn't said anything, he thought.

McQueen drew up a chair and sat down. Hamish sat down again next to him. "I have just suffered a visit from your constable," said McQueen. "He dared to suggest that my wife beats me."

"And does she?" asked Hamish baldly.

"My dear fellow, don't be silly."

"Yes, let's have a pleasant lunch," said Mary. While McQueen ordered food and drank some of her bottle of wine, Mary began to talk to him in "councilese" about diversity targets and meaningful interfaces with this or that person.

Hamish stopped listening, and his thoughts turned to Gloria McQueen. A woman who could so ruthlessly destroy those silver birches could well have attempted to sabotage the glen.

Then he started to listen again because McQueen was talking about his wife. "Instead of working her up the wrong way, Macbeth — aye, she told me you'd been to see her — she said she might have been able to give you some information. She was over at Drim just before the murders."

"What did she see or hear?" demanded

157

Hamish sharply.

"I forget what it was now," said McQueen. "This is grand wine, Mary."

Hamish stood up abruptly. "I've got to go," he said.

"But you haven't even finished your sandwich!" cried Mary.

"Thanks for lunch. Mr. McQueen, I might call on you later."

Hamish drove back up to the McQueens' villa. There was no sound of the chain saw that he could hear. He rang the doorbell and, after waiting for a few minutes, decided to walk round to the garden at the back. It was a beautiful day, and he wished with all his heart that the murder could be solved and that he would be once more free to laze around and enjoy the beauty of the countryside.

Once in the back garden, he froze with horror, barely able to believe the sight that met his eyes.

Gloria McQueen's dead head had been placed on the bole of one of the fallen silver birches. Her body lay some feet away. There was blood sprayed everywhere, turning the leaves on the fallen trees into a macabre travesty of autumn.

He backed away carefully so as not to

compromise the crime scene and phoned Jimmy. Then he phoned Dick and went out to the front of the house to wait.

What had Gloria seen over at Drim? She must have phoned someone as soon as he had left. He guessed she enjoyed power, and meeting him must have jolted her memory.

Like the murder of Mrs. Colchester, he was sure this was a hate crime.

CHAPTER SEVEN

Nature is not a temple, but a workshop,
and man's the workman in it.
— Ivan Turgenev

Jimmy Anderson, for once, behaved almost
as badly as his superior, Detective Chief
Inspector Blair. He rounded on Hamish in
a fury after getting the details of his meeting with Gloria.

"Thon dead woman was obviously killed
because she had important information," he
raged, "and all you could do was stand there
like a tumshie and ask her if she'd been
beating her husband. I checked the phone
in the house. She hadn't received any calls
but she must have phoned someone."

"She may not have used the phone in the
house," said Hamish. "I've a feeling she
didn't move from the garden. She may have
used her mobile."

Jimmy strode over to the tent that had

160

been erected over the crime scene and asked if a mobile phone had been found. There was a long silence and then a voice shouted, "No."

"Everyone's got one nowadays," said Hamish. "Ask the husband."

"It sounds as if he's arrived," said Jimmy as a great wail coming from the front of the house filled the air. "I'll see to it. Get back to your police station and type out a report about your interview with Gloria. I'll find out where the husband was."

"I left him in the pub with Mary," said Hamish. He quickly described how, following Jimmy's instructions, he had agreed to have lunch with Mary and then the provost had joined them.

He and Jimmy walked round to the front of the house. Blair had just arrived with Superintendent Daviot. McQueen was being comforted by Mary.

Jimmy, suddenly diminished by having his superiors on the scene, said in a quiet voice to Hamish, "You run along. I'll phone you later. When you've done your report, start checking alibis, Mary's brothers for a start, and then see what the wardens were doing."

Dick joined Hamish, who quickly told him what had happened and then said, "I've got to type up my report. Get over to the glen and get the brothers' alibis, though mind you, we'll be tripping over policemen all day long. There'll be so many coppers checking alibis, you might find they've been there before you."

Back at the police station, Hamish sat down in front of the computer and sighed. He had chosen to remain a humble village copper. So it was all his fault if he was once more removed from the heart of any investigation. He began to type, starting off by explaining the reason for his visit. He vividly remembered the felled silver birches and Gloria's flushed face. An easy woman to hate. But to be killed in such a way! Someone even had the nerve to display the severed head on the tree bole.

And what were the "some things" she had been referring to?

He sent over his report, collected his dog and cat, and got back into his Land Rover. He decided to call on the Palfours. Was it possible they could have killed Mrs. Colchester? But why? Had they known about the will all along? But if they had, it would have been more in their interest to keep the old woman alive and try to cajole her into changing her will.

Ralph Palfour answered the door. "What

is it now?" he demanded.

"Have you already had a visit from the police?" asked Hamish.

"No. Your superiors have had the decency to leave us alone."

"There's been a new and horrible development," said Hamish. "May I come in?"

"If you must. The hall here will do. What is this new development?"

Hamish told him of the gruesome murder of Gloria McQueen.

He clutched onto a chair back. "There's a maniac on the loose," he gasped.

"You must understand," said Hamish, "that we have to eliminate people from our enquiries. Where were you this lunchtime?"

"My wife and I were returning from Inverness. An auctioneer is coming up to look at the furniture. Let me see. Lunchtime? We'd be back here."

"Is there anyone who can vouch for that?" asked Hamish. "Your cleaners?"

"It's their day off."

"And the children?"

"At school. They're settling down. The school takes boarders. We may board them when we sell this place and leave for London."

"Did you receive any phone calls since you came back?"

"Only one, from Sotheby's. We're selling off a lot of the contents of the strong room."

"I would like to take a statement from your wife."

"She's lying down at the moment."

"I will come back later then," said Hamish doggedly.

Instead of going to the glen to see how Dick was getting on, Hamish, after he had left the hunting box, parked up a heathery farm track. He wanted peace and quiet to think.

The press would be soon descending in hordes, bringing the outside world to Sutherland. Hamish's hatred of the murderer or murderers grew. Sutherland stretches over much of Scotland's far north and is one of the most sparsely populated areas of Britain — and perhaps, the most beautiful. It usually has a sense of peace because it is too remote to be blighted by crowds of tourists. Giant monolithic mountains are reflected in blue lochs. In fact, it contains all the charm and beauty that kept Hamish Macbeth determined to stay anchored to his police station.

Surely it had all started with the shattering of that peace the moment the glen was turned into a tourist attraction, a sort of Pandora's box which had been opened to let the gawking sightseers in. When he was out of Mary's orbit, Hamish found he rather disliked her and yes, there was something vulgar about her. True, she had brought much-needed business into the town, but at what cost?

And the Palfours with their peculiarly *shuttered* air and their emotionally damaged children. What of them? They were a sort of canker on the place. He got down from the Land Rover and let the dog and cat out to run and play. Then he opened cans of food and fed them before getting them back into the vehicle and driving off.

As he arrived at the entrance to the glen, he saw, as he got down from the Land Rover, an unmarked police car heading towards the hunting box. There would be no need to go back for Fern Palfour's statement, he thought ruefully. Bullying Blair was on the job.

Dick and the brothers were seated on camp chairs drinking tea. Dick hailed him with, "They've been here all the time and that Mrs. Timoty over by the turnstile can vouch for them."

"Where are the wardens?"

"They'll be patrolling the glen," said Brad Brooke.

Two tour buses were parked outside as well as many cars. "There're lots o' polis in the glen," said Brad cheerfully. "They're seeing if one of the tourists could be a mad psycho. In fact, they'd already had statements from us before your man here arrived."

"No use us going over the same ground, Dick," said Hamish. "Walk with me for a bit until I think what to do."

He led Dick over to where he had parked the Land Rover. "To tell the truth," said Hamish, "I don't know where to begin. I don't want to interview people who have already been interviewed. Gloria's neighbours, for example. The police will already have questioned them. Maybe her death has nothing to do with any of the other stuff. Maybe McQueen had had enough and nipped back home and took the chain saw to her. But she'd be too powerful for him and I can't see that he would have had the time. Anyway, whoever killed her would be covered in blood.

"And who stole the stuff out of the strong room? You would think it would have to be the Palfours, but they did seem genuinely shocked and furious over the missing items."

"I happen to know from a friend in Strathbane that the cleaners' houses were searched from top to bottom and even their gardens were dug up," said Dick, "so it doesn't look as if it could be one o' them."

"I'm going back to Lochdubh to go through my notes," said Hamish. "All that'll happen today, Dick, is that we'll be tripping over policemen and all of us asking the same questions."

Back at the police station, Hamish went into his office and patiently began to read piles of notes, marking down all the likely suspects, his mind searching all the time for clues.

By late afternoon, he decided to take the dog and cat out for a breath of fresh air before Jimmy arrived.

His friend Angela Brodie, the doctor's wife, joined him on the waterfront. "It's a black day for the neighbourhood, Hamish," she said. "It's scary. Out there is some homicidal maniac. I got a call from a friend in Braikie and the whole place is swarming with police and press. Will Elspeth be back?"

"Maybe."

"Have you seen Priscilla?"

"She interrupted my dinner with Mary the other night." Hamish realised with a little shock that he had not thought of her once since then. "Jimmy is coming over the night to see me. I might take a run up to the hotel afterwards."

Hamish saw Jimmy's car driving up to the police station and hurried back to meet him.

"I'm fair exhausted," said Jimmy. "Got any whisky?"

"Aye, sit yourself down and I'll get the bottle and a glass."

"Where's your sidekick?"

"I don't know," said Hamish.

"Isn't that a note on the dishwasher?"

"So it is." Hamish unfolded a piece of notepaper. It was only a brief message. "Gone to Aberdeen. Back late. Dick."

"What on earth has he gone all the way to Aberdeen for?" asked Hamish.

Jimmy grinned. "I think I know. There's a quiz programme on Grampian TV tonight. The prize is a flat-screen TV."

"If he wins, I'll neffer get any work out of the man," moaned Hamish. "Any new developments?"

"Nothing but plod, plod, plod, checking alibis down to the last minute. Blair's pawing the ground like an enraged bull, desperate to arrest anyone at all. Daviot had to stop him from hauling in the provost. The fact that you seem to be the provost's alibi just made him worse. I'm beginning to wonder if it's all because of the old woman's will or if there really is some schizo out on the loose we don't know about."

"Was she hit on the head or drugged?"

"Bashed on the head. How did you guess?"

"Easy. There were no signs of a desperate struggle and she had no defensive wounds. I was going over my notes and there is just one thing. There are these two boys, Callum and Rory Macgregor. They were down at the pool during the night, having slipped out. They said they saw the fairies — dancing lights and a voice telling them to go away. I'd like another word with them. It'll get them in bad with their parents but I'm clutching at straws. I might just call this evening. I have their address."

Jimmy drained his glass. "Well, off you go, because right at this moment I haven't anything for you."

It was only when he was driving along the shore road to Braikie that Hamish realised he had forgotten his plan of calling at the hotel to see Priscilla. Maybe he was completely free of her at last.

He parked outside the boys' home on the council estate, walked up the brick path, and rang the doorbell. A trim little woman answered the door, her hand flying to her breast in alarm when she saw his uniform. "My husband!"

"No, nothing bad. I just wanted a wee word with your boys."

"They're good boys."

"Yes, yes," said Hamish patiently. "It'll only take a moment."

She ushered him into the living room where Callum and Rory were doing their homework. School again, thought Hamish bleakly. The end of summer.

They threw Hamish anguished looks. "You promised," said Callum.

"I know," said Hamish. "But you'll have heard about this awful murder. I need your help."

"How can my boys help you?" demanded their mother.

"It's like this," said Hamish. "Boys will be boys and one night they sneaked out and went down to the glen and saw something. I need to ask them again what they saw."

"Wait until your father hears about this!" exclaimed Mrs. Macgregor.

The boys looked guilty and miserable.

Hamish sat down at the table next to them. "Now, I want you two to play detective," he said. "I'm sure your parents would want you to help the police. So what was it you saw and heard?"

Rory said, "It was right dark but when we got to the glen, there were little flashing lights and we got scared. Then a deep voice told us to go away and we ran for it."

"When you ran out of the glen, did you see anyone?"

"Nobody," said Rory. "But we were scared and running hard."

"Did you hear anything?"

"Just a squeaky noise."

"Like an animal? Like what?"

"Like the front wheel o' my bike when it had a sair dunt. It went squeak, a bit like that noise I heard."

"I'm going to type up what you said and get you to sign it," said Hamish. "It may be important."

"You mean like we're real detectives?" said Rory.

"I think you'd make the grand detectives," said Hamish.

"Don't you be encouraging them!" declared Mrs. Macgregor.

"And don't you be hard on them," said Hamish.

Back at the police station, he went into the office and studied what the boys had said. An idea was beginning to form inside his head. Mrs. Colchester had believed Mary's story of having the second sight. She was brought up on Rosse and was surely superstitious. All those valuables had disappeared from the strong room. People who believed in fairies, believed in placating them.

Rowan trees, meant to ward them off, were still planted outside cottage doors. Some old people still put out saucers of milk at night for the fairies. In the west of Scotland, the old beliefs died hard.

He clutched his red hair and stared at the notes. Just suppose Mary had promised Mrs. Colchester safety from a hard and long life. Perhaps she had persuaded the gullible old woman to take items from the strong room to the glen and place them somewhere. Then she and her brothers would collect them. Maybe Mrs. Colchester had wised up to them and said she was going to change her will.

Perhaps Mary was keeping the precious items until the fuss died down.

But how to get a search warrant for her house and her brothers' house? He phoned Jimmy and expounded his theory.

"I think thon trip to that island has made you as daft as thae brothers," scoffed Jimmy. "What do you think the sheriff would say if I went to him wi' your ridiculous story? Have you been drinking?"

"No, I have not," yelled Hamish. "And what's more I'll send over a report on this."

"Well, get a good night's sleep and look forward to your new telly."

"You mean he won?" asked Hamish, momentarily diverted.

"Hands down."

When Jimmy had rung off, Hamish sat deep in thought. He would phone Mary in the morning and see if he could meet her for lunch again. He would bring the conversation round to people who still thought the fairies ought to be placated and see her reaction. He typed out his report and sent it.

But before he could phone in the morning, he received a call from Detective Chief Inspector Blair.

Blair was furious with frustration. The press were hounding the police, and Jimmy had to pull him back before he punched a photographer. He wanted to vent his feelings and he hated Hamish. Hamish listened patiently to the diatribe until it was interrupted by Blair's phone ringing. From the suddenly crawling note in Blair's voice, Hamish guessed it was Daviot on the line.

When Blair rang off, he simply darted out of the police station, slamming the door behind him.

Hamish phoned Mary. She said she would

be delighted to meet him in the pub at one o'clock. Remembering Priscilla at last, he phoned the Tommel Castle Hotel, relieved when her cool voice came on the line.

"I wonder if I can come and see you. There's an idea I've got."

Priscilla sounded amused. "And you want me to be Watson?"

"Just wanted to run an idea past you."

"All right. Come along. I'll have the coffee ready."

Before he left, Hamish had a look in Dick's bedroom. The constable was fast sleep. Hamish decided not to rouse him.

At the hotel, he outlined his idea of placating the fairies to Priscilla and waited anxiously. She looked as calm and elegant as ever, the bell of her fair hair framing her perfect face.

"It's far-fetched," she said, "but you've got nothing else to go on, have you? I mean, why did the old woman go down to the pool during the night? They say the legends about the fairies started a long, long time ago. People believe there was once a race of small people up here who were driven underground by the larger humans. Some people in the more isolated areas still bury iron and salt outside their croft houses to keep the bad fairies away. But when you put your theory to Mary and she doesn't react, what will you do? And even if she looks guilty, you're still not going to get a search warrant on the strength of that."

"I wish I hadn't sent that report," said Hamish gloomily. "If Blair gets hold of it, he'll take it straight to Daviot with proof that I should be kept off the case."

Daviot received a phone call from his wife. "Do you know what Rona has done now?" demanded his wife. She did not use the strangulated refined accents she used in speaking to someone like Priscilla when calling her husband. Daviot repressed a sigh. Rona was their maid, and the last thing he wanted to hear in the middle of a murder enquiry were more complaints about Rona, a squat young female from the Outer Hebrides, but he knew better than to cut his wife off. "She broke my best vase," said Mrs. Daviot, "and now she's saying it wasn't her, it was the fairies. She says it's because I stopped her putting iron in the garden to keep them away. I'd fire her but she's usually good. The trouble is she's shaken and really seems to believe it."

"There are a lot of the old superstitions still around," said Daviot. "I'll get you a new vase. Don't worry. She cooks like a dream. You won't get anyone near as good."

His secretary Helen appeared in the doorway as he was ringing off. "Mr. Blair to see you, sir," said Helen, her usually sour face looking cheerful for once. Blair had told her that Hamish had run mad and Daviot was going to be furious. Helen detested Hamish.

"You must see this daft report from Macbeth," chortled Blair. "The man should be suspended from duty immediately." Daviot began to read while Blair watched him avidly.

The smile died on Blair's face as he saw that Daviot was carefully reading the report twice. At last he laid it down. "I'm going to try to get search warrants," he said. "It will be difficult but I am sure Macbeth has something here worth looking into."

"But surely, sir, you cannae . . ."

"That will be all. I will let you know." Daviot picked up the phone and waved his hand to dismiss Blair, who stomped out and then went straight to the pub to confide in a bored barman that even his boss had gone mad.

Mary was wearing a kingfisher-blue dress. She smiled charmingly at Hamish after they had placed their orders for lunch and said coyly, "Now tell me, why were you so anxious to see me?"

Hamish's hazel eyes were serious. "It's like this, Mary. What if someone knew that Mrs. Colchester was superstitious and persuaded her that the fairies had to be placated? She went out during the night in her wheelchair. A show was laid on for her. Sparkling lights and eerie voices. She was told to put her silver and gold and jewels in the pool over several nights, probably at that shallow bit. Then they could be recovered. But she got wise to the trick and said she was going to change her will."

Something glinted in Mary's eyes like the flash of a kingfisher's wing, and then she gave a laugh. "I've never heard anything more ridiculous."

Hamish's mobile phone rang. It was Jimmy. "I don't know how you did it," he said, "but we're heading over to Braikie with search warrants."

"We'd better go," said Hamish to Mary. "There are search warrants for your house and your brothers' house."

Startled, she rose to her feet. "I'd better be there. Such nonsense."

"I'll come with you."

"I prefer to be on my own. This is your

fault, Hamish. I *trusted* you."

Hamish was about to hurry after her when he noticed the waiter barring his way and holding out a bill. He paid for their meals and then rushed out. No sign of Mary. He walked to where his Land Rover was parked, checked Mary's address, and drove there as quickly as possible.

Her home was a neat bungalow on the shore road. Hamish thought she had probably got it cheap because prices on the road were still low, people not trusting the new seawall to keep them from flooding.

The brothers' home was in the bungalow next door. He had driven quickly. He saw Mary on the doorstep, just about to enter. Then police cars drove up, an unmarked one holding Blair and Jimmy leading the procession.

Hamish got down from the Land Rover and would have joined them, but Blair snarled, "You! Keep away." Hamish stood on the other side of the road.

Mary was led out and stood on the doorstep, her eyes full of tears. Another police car rolled up and then the brothers got out, looking furious. One search squad went into Mary's house and another into the brothers' home.

Soon the road began to fill up with press

and onlookers. Hamish stood and waited. The sun was hot on his head and yet under the warmth he could feel the cold fingers of approaching autumn. The rowan tree at Mary's door was bent down under the weight of scarlet berries. The search went on for two hours. Mary was sitting on the doorstep. She looked across at Hamish, and he could have sworn her blue eyes were mocking him.

Blair and Jimmy were pacing up and down outside, letting the search teams get on with their work.

Hamish studied the rowan tree. He fished out a strong pair of binoculars. He noticed that the ground around the rowan tree had recently been paved with squares of new turf.

He knew if he crossed the road, Blair would not listen to him and would send him away. He phoned Jimmy's mobile and when the detective answered, he said, "Have a look under the rowan tree. There's new turf there. Why?"

He saw Jimmy go into the house. Mary looked across at Hamish with an odd pleading look on her face.

Soon men started digging under the rowan. Then one of them bent down and hauled up a leather bag and opened it. Mary began to scream. Jimmy looked across at Hamish and gave him the thumbs-up.

Mary and her brothers were arrested. To Hamish's surprise, Jimmy had given him the credit for finding the valuables. Although Jimmy was not nearly as bad as Blair, he still often liked to take the praise for one of Hamish's ideas. Daviot phoned later when Hamish was back in Lochdubh to congratulate Hamish, saying, "Well, that wraps it all up. They'll be charged with the murder of Mrs. Colchester and Mrs. McQueen as well."

"I don't know about the murders, sir," said Hamish cautiously. "There's proof that the brothers at the time of Gloria McQueen's murder were building the gift shop and Mary was with me. If they get a good defence lawyer, they'll get off."

"We'll find evidence," snapped Daviot. "The brothers swear their sister had nothing to do with it. But we've got her husband in custody as well. Don't you see? He's got no alibi. But if the brothers stick to their story, we'll have to release Mary."

"But . . . ," began Hamish, but Daviot had rung off.

Hamish sat deep in thought. He could not help feeling uneasy. He wished with all his

180

heart they would find some proof that the brothers had murdered the two women. He was sure they had tricked the superstitious Mrs. Colchester until she had come to her senses. He wondered how long they would keep Mary for questioning.

He was sitting in his office when a blast of sound from his living room reached his ears. He realised he had gone straight into his office without giving Dick the news.

Dick was in the living room, his chubby hands clutching a remote control. A large new flat-screen television dominated the room. "Turn the sound down," yelled Hamish.

Dick, looking like a sulky child, switched off the television. "I thought you'd be pleased," he said.

"Listen to the latest news," said Hamish impatiently.

"Right," said Dick, switching on the television set again.

"No!" yelled Hamish. "I mean my news about the murders."

"Oh, I heard that. The brothers have been pulled in. They found those valuables in the garden."

"How did you know that?" asked Hamish.

"The Currie sisters called by when you were out and told me all about it."

181

"I should just leave you to do all the detecting from the living room. I've got to go through my notes. There's something I'm missing."

Dick held up the remote control and pleaded, "Can I just hae a wee keek?"

"Aye, but keep the sound down. Oh, and congratulations."

Dick grinned happily and switched the box back on.

Hamish fretted over his notes. He wished the Palfours didn't have such cast-iron alibis. When Gloria was being murdered, they had been filmed on CCTV at a garage halfway from Inverness. If the brothers weren't behind the murders, someone else was. Mary was not innocent. She must be very naive, thought Hamish. Hadn't she realised that the police would be sure to dig up the garden? Maybe in her way she was as superstitious as Mrs. Colchester and thought the rowan tree would protect her. She had a powerful effect on people, and he felt that the brothers and her husband were prepared to take the rap to protect her.

Hamish decided to go back to the quarry to see if he could find anything he might have missed. It was what they euphemistically call in the Highlands "a nice soft day." A thin drizzle was shrouding the landscape, and the mountains seem to have disappeared. Everything was grey.

Hamish climbed down into the quarry and painstakingly started to search it from one end to the other. He finally found only a discarded cigarette end under a gorse bush. He carefully bagged it, wondering if he would ever get permission to send it away to get tested for DNA. Daviot, he knew, was tired of pressure from the press and wanted the cases of murder wrapped up. Hamish thought, as he had in the past, that Daviot and Blair were as bad as politicians when it came to spin: anything for a decent headline and to send the press home. Hamish could only be glad that no one got hanged any more in Scotland.

Nonetheless, it might be worth a try. He phoned Jimmy and explained what he had found.

"You know how it goes," said Jimmy wearily. "Daviot's like a peacock, strutting in front of the press. As far as he is concerned, that's the end of it."

"But surely the brothers, Mary Leinster, and her husband are not admitting to the murders?"

"No, but get this. The brothers and Tim

Leinster have put their hands up to robbing Mrs. Colchester and have signed written statements to say Mary had nothing to do with it. They said that Mary really believed she had the second sight and so they pushed Charles into the pool to make her prophecy come true. Then they sabotaged the bridge to persuade Mrs. Colchester that the fairies needed further placating. They also confess to killing the kingfisher. But they refuse to confess to either of the two murders. But get this. Mary is out. She's got some expensive defence lawyer and there's nothing to hold her on."

"Surely Blair didn't allow a lawyer to see her?"

In Scotland, it is the police's decision as to whether the accused can see a lawyer or not, although the Scottish Parliament is suggesting a change in the law.

"She fainted, or staged a faint, and she cried and cried. Blair got alarmed and let her have her lawyer and that was that. Bag that cigarette anyway. It doesn't matter what Daviot says. He's going to realise soon that they haven't enough evidence to charge them with the murders and it'll be back to square one. Drop the evidence at police headquarters."

Hamish climbed back up the quarry as a

watery beam of sunlight shone down. The mist began to roll up the mountains, a sight which never stopped fascinating him. How old these mountains were! One and a half billion years! Scientists over at Lochinver had discovered microbes in the rocks that might prove how life began on earth.

He drove to police headquarters in Strathbane. The town seemed filthier and dingier than ever, a blot on the beauty of the west of Scotland. If they ever closed his police station, they would expect Hamish to move into the town and work there. "Over my dead body," he muttered.

He left the evidence bag at the desk. "See that Detective Anderson gets that," he said.

"I thought the case was closed," said the desk sergeant. "This can't have anything to do with the murders."

"It might," said Hamish, and turned and left.

Outside headquarters, Blair suspiciously watched Hamish's retreating back. He went inside and asked the desk sergeant, "What did that teuchter, Macbeth, want?"

"Just leaving a bit of evidence for Anderson. It's to do with the murders," said the desk sergeant.

Blair stiffened. The murder cases were solved and that was that. No highland copper was going to stop it. He reached out one fat, mottled, hairy hand. "I'll take it."

Once inside, he shoved the evidence bag in his pocket.

The noise of the new television set reached Hamish's ears when he entered the police station in Lochdubh. He went in to the living room, seized the remote control from Dick, and said, "You're supposed to be working."

"I'd only just started to hae a look," said Dick petulantly. "Thon bonnie lassie, Elspeth, was here looking for you."

"She's still up here?"

"She heard that Mary Leinster had been released and she's off to hae a word with her."

"Come on, then," urged Hamish. "Let's see if we can talk to her ourselves."

As Hamish went out to the Land Rover, he could see a couple of tourists, husband and wife, shouting at each other on the waterfront.

"Was this your idea of a holiday?" yelled the woman. Her accent was English. "Why did you drag me up to this godforsaken hole? I don't care if we've got two days left. I want to go home."

The sky had started to cloud over again, and rain was weeping down.

"Nothing ever pleases you," said her husband. He was a middle-aged man with brown hair, dressed in knee breeches and a tweed jacket. His wife was scrawny and wearing tight jeans, a Barbour coat, and high heels.

"Oh, get lost," she screamed, "and while you're at it, as our Australian cousins say, why don't you stuff your head up a dead bear's bum?"

"And to think," said Hamish as they drove off, "that folks will keep telling me I'd be happier if I were married."

"Ah, but ye wouldnae need to marry someone like thon one," said Dick. "What about Elspeth Grant?"

"Mind your own business!"

When Hamish reached the shore road, it was to find a crowd of reporters and television crews being addressed by a silver-haired man whom Hamish recognised as being one of Edinburgh's top defence lawyers, James Farquhar-Symondson.

"And that is the end of my statement," he was saying as Hamish approached. "There will be no interviews. Mrs. Leinster has had a bad shock and needs to recover."

Elspeth turned round and saw Hamish. She said something to her crew and then went to join him.

Hamish stared at her. Elspeth was glowing. Her straightened hair was shining, and her grey eyes sparkled like silver in the weak sunlight.

"Let's go somewhere quiet," said Elspeth. "Quick. Into the Land Rover. The others have just spotted you."

They drove off before the other reporters could reach them. "Can you lose them?" asked Elspeth.

"Easily," said Hamish.

He drove through the town and then urged the vehicle off the road and bumped over the moors before rejoining the road again.

"That's lost them," said Hamish, looking in the rearview mirror. "There's a wee café at Craskie. We can go there."

Once seated in the café — pie and chips for Dick, coffees for Hamish and Elspeth — Hamish said, "You're looking grand, Elspeth."

"Aye," agreed Dick. "Who is he, Elspeth?"

"What?" A rosy blush crept up Elspeth's cheeks.

"I can tell the signs," said Dick, while Hamish glared at him.

"If you must know," said Elspeth, "it's the head of news, a new guy, Barry Darymple. We're going to be married."

"When?" asked Dick, as Hamish felt a grey depression settling on him.

"Next spring." She flicked an odd sort of sly look at Hamish. "You'll both come to my wedding, of course."

"Grand," said Hamish bleakly, thinking that all women were the same: every man they let go of ended up with claw marks on him. He knew Elspeth was hoping her news hurt him. Well, he had so many times been on the point of proposing to her and something always came up to stop him.

"Anyway, never mind that," said Elspeth. "I suppose it means that the Palfours are going to be very rich indeed."

"Do you know, I never thought of that," said Hamish. "Of course, the Leinsters cannot profit by a criminal act. There's not enough to charge them with murder, but it means that Mrs. Colchester's will goes back to a previous one. There is a previous one, I know."

"I checked that," said Elspeth. "Before she changed her will, the old will left everything to her daughter. Now, there's a motive."

"I don't see it," said Hamish. "If the Palfours knew that the brothers and Tim Leir

189

ster were conning the old girl out of her valuables, they'd have gone to the police. I think Mrs. Colchester found out about the trick and didn't tell anyone for fear of looking ridiculous — or rather, she probably told Mary and said she was changing her will."

"So you think Mary is actually guilty?" asked Elspeth.

"I cannot believe she knew nothing about it," said Hamish.

"Dear me," commented Elspeth. "I thought those big blue eyes had blinded you."

"Miaow!" mumbled Dick through a mouthful of pie and Elspeth glared at him.

"I wonder how I can get to speak to her," said Hamish.

Dick finished his pie and said, "That one had a soft spot for ye."

"I doubt that," said Hamish. "She was probably cosying up to me to find out as much as she could." Now he was away from Mary, he saw her as shallow and manipulative and wondered how he had ever found her attractive.

"That lawyer can't stay with her forever," said Elspeth. "I've got to get back to Glasgow."

"Aren't you staying for the prelim at the

sheriff's court?" asked Hamish.

"I don't dare. Every woman seems to want my job and they go after it as soon as I'm out of the studio."

"Having the head of news as a fiancé must help," said Hamish sourly.

"I still don't trust them," said Elspeth.

"Where will you be getting married?" asked Dick.

"I've spoken to the minister, Mr. Wellington. I'm going to be married in Lochdubh."

And I'll be off on holiday when you do, thought Hamish.

He drove up to the hunting box, remembering his conversation with Annie, and wondering if he could have a talk with the children. They were seated on the terrace, schoolbooks spread out on the table in front of them.

"You seem to have settled in well at your new school," said Hamish.

Olivia studied him for a moment. "You should not be speaking to us without an adult present," she said primly.

"Just a wee chat," said Hamish. "We never found thon schoolteacher who assaulted you. Must have been a traumatic experience."

Olivia stifled a yawn. "He'll turn up

somewhere. All those paedophiles are registered on the Net if you know where to look."

Hamish studied her for a long moment. He was suddenly sure that they had found out the teacher's background and used it when they thought it might come in useful. Or had they been blackmailing him?

"I do not think you were assaulted at all," he said.

Olivia's face became contorted with fear. "I'll report you," she screamed.

Hamish touched his cap. "Good day to you. But remember, if he's caught, you'll have a lot of explaining to do."

As he walked away, he was sure they had made up the whole story. What other lies had they told?

CHAPTER EIGHT

Alas, how easily things go wrong!
A sigh too much, or a kiss too long,
And there follows a mist and a weeping
  rain,
And life is never the same again.
                    — George Macdonald

A month passed after the brothers and Tim
Leinster were scheduled to appear at the
High Court in Edinburgh the following
year. The early frosts appeared in the mornings. And all that month, Mary refused to
answer the phone and kept to her house.

Apart from occasional forays to try to see
Mary, Hamish tried to go about his beat as
usual. He learned that the Palfours were
still in Braikie, waiting for the will to be an-
nulled.

Then one morning, Jimmy called on him.

"Come in," said Hamish eagerly. "Any
news?"

"Only the bad news I think you've been expecting. They have at last decided there isn't enough to charge thae bastards with the murders so we're back to square one. So where's that cigarette end you picked up in the quarry?"

"I left it in an evidence bag with the desk sergeant."

"Aye, he confirms that. Can you stop that cat of yours from staring at me? It gives me the creeps."

"Sonsie's just looking. So where's the evidence gone?"

"The desk sergeant says that Blair took it. Blair swears he left it on my desk."

"Aha!"

"Aha, what?"

"I bet he took it."

"Why would he?"

"Come on, Jimmy, think! As far as the fat fool was concerned, the murders were all wrapped up. He didn't want anything spoiling his moment of glory."

"I can hardly accuse him of stealing it with Daviot backing him up. Anyway, Mary's had to call her lawyer again. Everyone's got to be interviewed all over again."

"I'll take the Palfours," said Hamish.

"You can't. Blair doesn't want you to have anything to do with the case. He's found

194

out you had dinner with Mary and then you had lunch with her. He's persuaded Daviot that your views on the murders are therefore skewed. Sorry, Hamish. I've got to get off. I'm not supposed to be here."

After he had left, Hamish sat in the kitchen with the heavy wild cat on his lap and his dog at his feet.

Then he finally had an idea. "Come on, folks," he said to his pets. "We're going visiting."

First, he drove to Strathbane dressed in civilian clothes with a black woollen hat pulled down over his flaming red hair. He walked to police headquarters and checked the car park. He saw Blair's driver's car parked there.

He then drove to Blair's home, went up to the door, and rang the bell. Mrs. Blair answered the door, her face lighting up when she saw Hamish. She was an ex-prostitute whom Hamish had helped con Blair into marriage. Mrs. Blair now looked the epitome of tweedy respectability. No one could understand how she coped with her awful husband, but Mrs. Blair enjoyed being married and dealing with Blair, she found, was little trouble compared with what she had to go through when she was on the game.

"Come ben, Hamish," she said. "What brings you?"

Hamish followed her into a cosy living room. It was clean and comfortable with a small coal fire burning on the hearth.

"Tea? Coffee?"

"Maybe later," said Hamish. "I found a piece of evidence and I think your husband nicked it."

Mrs. Blair did not look in the least surprised. "He wouldn't bring it home, would he?"

"He chust might," said Hamish, made nervous by hope. "Where would he put it?"

"Come through to the bedroom. He might have left it in one of his pockets."

"I shouldnae think so," said Hamish. "The man only has the one suit."

"That's where you're wrong. He's got six of them, all the same."

"Why?"

"If you're a heavy drinker like my man and always dropping food on your clothes or puking on them, you need more than just the one."

Hamish followed her into the bedroom. She swung open the doors of an old-fashioned mahogany wardrobe. Five suits were hanging along with two sports jackets and an anorak. "Heffens!" exclaimed Hamish. "Quite the dandy."

"I wouldn't call wearing the same cut of suit over and over again being a dandy," said Mrs. Blair. "I'll leave you to it."

Hamish diligently searched through all the pockets without success. He searched the shelf above the clothes but found nothing there. He went through the bedside tables, but there was no sign of any evidence bag.

Frustrated and made angry by failure, he wrenched the mattress off the bed. The evidence bag fell to the floor.

"Got him!" cried Hamish.

Mrs. Blair came hurrying back in and looked in alarm at the evidence bag in Hamish's hand.

"Look here, Hamish," she pleaded. "I don't want him out of a job."

"I'll tell you what I'll do," said Hamish. "I'll find a way to get this to Jimmy. I won't mention I found it here. Now, what about a coffee?"

Hamish drove back to Lochdubh and changed into his uniform. He said to Sonsie and Lugs, "Look after yourselves and don't get up to any mischief," and then set off for Strathbane again.

Again he checked the car park. Blair's car

was no longer there.

He went into police headquarters and got buzzed through to the detectives' room. It was empty. He went straight to Jimmy's desk and put the evidence bag in his top drawer. Then he phoned Jimmy on his mobile. Jimmy and Blair were being driven to Braikie to interview the Palfours.

"I've found that bit o' missing evidence," said Hamish. "You'll never guess where it was?"

"Where?"

"Caught down the side of the top drawer of your desk. You'll now find it in the top drawer."

"Grand. As soon as I'm back I'll get it over to the lab," said Jimmy.

"What was that all about?" asked Blair when Jimmy had rung off.

Jimmy told him.

"Whit!" roared Blair, beginning to sweat. "Why can't thon bugger keep to his damn sheep?"

When they arrived at the Palfours' home, Blair said to Jimmy, "You go ahead. I've left some important notes in Strathbane."

"Send the driver, sir," suggested Jimmy.

"Look! Do as you're told."

As soon as Blair had been driven off, Jimmy phoned Annie Williams. "Do me a favour," he said. "In the top drawer of my desk, you'll find an evidence bag. Send it over to the lab for a rush job."

Blair hurtled into police headquarters and went straight to Jimmy's desk. When he didn't find anything, he phoned the lab. "Have you just received an evidence bag?" he asked.

"Aye, came in a half hour go," said a lab technician.

Blair cursed and rang off. He got his driver to take him home.

The minute he let himself in he confronted his wife, who was knitting placidly. "Was Macbeth here?" he demanded.

"Yes, why?"

"Did you let him search the place?"

His wife looked at him in well-feigned amazement. "Why would he do that? I had to go out to the shop for some more wool and I left him to make himself some coffee. He was gone when I got back."

Blair sat down heavily and put his head in his hands. For some reason, Hamish had covered up for him after finding the evidence bag. So now he was in the awful position of being in debt to Hamish Macbeth.

If you can't beat them, join them, thought

Hamish, settling down in front of the television that evening with a cup of coffee. Dick was watching a game show. The sound was rather loud and at first Hamish did not hear the phone ring. When he did, he shouted to Dick to turn the sound down and ran through to the office.

He got a jolt of surprise to hear Mary's voice on the phone. "I can't take any more, Hamish," she sobbed. "I've got to speak to you. I'm frightened."

"I'll come now," said Hamish.

"No, tomorrow," whispered Mary. "Out of the village. Meet me up on Bracken Brae." Bracken Brae was a heathery rise outside Braikie a little to the north.

"What time?" asked Hamish.

"Noon. Don't tell anybody, please."

"All right," said Hamish. "See you then."

When he rang off, he experienced a surge of excitement. Perhaps she might be able to tell him something that might break the case.

Callum and Rory Macgregor shared a bedroom. When their mother thought they were both asleep, Callum lit a torch and whispered, "Are you awake, Rory?"

"Aye."

"Well, I've been thinking. The bad yins

are all locked up. Thon lights in the glen were really pretty. I'd like to see a fairy."

Rory sat up in bed. "We could maybe catch one. We'd be famous."

"Let's go. Ma's asleep and I can hear Da snoring."

They quietly dressed and opened the window. Both nimbly slipped down the drainpipe and set off through the sleeping streets of Braikie under a full moon.

"Thae tourists have all gone," said Rory.

"What about the wardens?"

"I heard Da saying they were lazy and were probably asleep or down in the pub."

The boys climbed over the turnstile and entered the glen. A full moon rose overhead. Sutherland is one of the few places left in Britain where you can still see the heavens in all their glory. The sky was blazing with stars.

To their disappointment, the glen was dark and still. The moon was reflected in the pool.

"Och, we'd better forget it and go home," said Rory. "Nae fairies."

"Maybe another kingfisher's come."

"We cannae take any eggs," warned his brother. "But maybe we could see the birds asleep."

They made their way cautiously round the

edge of the pool to where the willow tree trailed its branches in the water. The leaves were turning yellow, and a few floated in the pool.

Rory was searching for a nest when Callum suddenly let out a shriek. "There's a fairy under the water!"

Callum came to stand by him and together they looked down into the moonlit pool.

"That's no fairy," said Callum beginning to shake. "That's that wumman, Mary Leinster."

"Come away," said Rory, "let's run for it."

But when they arrived home it was to find their father waiting by the garden gate, his arms folded.

"Where hae you two been?" he demanded.

Rory began to cry. Callum fell to his knees and holding himself with his arms, started to shake.

"Here now, lads," said Mr. Macgregor, "I'm no' a monster. Get to your beds."

"She's dead. Drowned," wailed Callum.

"Who? What?"

So Callum told him.

Hamish was awakened by the shrill ringing of the telephone. Even before he answered it, he experienced a feeling of dread.

He listened with a sinking heart to Mr. Macgregor's agitated voice, and then said grimly, "I'll be right over."

"What do you think happened?" Dick asked as they raced along the moonlit roads.

"I think Mary wanted money. Now that the valuables have been recovered and she would find it difficult to milk the trust, she wanted money somehow. She must have known something and thought she would try a bit of blackmail. I'll be interested to hear what the Palfours were doing when all this was going on."

They arrived at the pool to find Mary's body being lifted from the water, her hair dank and wet in the moonlight, her face like clay.

Jimmy saw Hamish and came hurrying up. "Go and talk to the lads who found the body and take Annie Williams with you."

"Where are the Palfours?"

"On the road back. They were staying at a hotel in Inverness, left the number with the cleaner. Stopped at a garage this morning for petrol. Got them on CCTV."

"So, again, they've got an alibi. Where are their children?"

"They're now boarding at their school during the week. I want you and Annie Williams here to go and speak to the boys. Annie! Come here. I want you to go with Macbeth. Dick, you stay and do some plod work. Search the area and see if you can find anything."

When Annie and Hamish reached the boys' home, it was to be told that they had been given sedatives by the doctor and were asleep in bed.

"Now what?" asked Annie as they got back into the Land Rover.

Hamish phoned Jimmy. "I don't need you here cluttering up the landscape," he said, "or rather, I'm quoting Blair. Annie can go home but you can come here first and pick up Dick. Mary Leinster was hit on the head with something and then shoved in the pool."

"I'm hungry," complained Annie as they set off for the glen again.

"Have you got a car?"

"I left mine and came over with the other police."

"Tell you what," said Hamish, "I'll drive us all back to Lochdubh and make sandwiches or something and then I'll run you home."

At the police station, Dick said he wanted to go straight to bed. Hamish made a pot of tea and some ham sandwiches.

"That was grand," said Annie. "Can you give me a bed for a few hours? We'll both have to see those boys later on."

"I'll take the bed in the cell and give you mine."

She gave him an impish grin. "Why don't we both share your bed?"

"Annie!"

She stood up and bent over him and gave him a passionate kiss on the mouth.

"Feeling better about the idea?" she asked.

"Oh, yes," said Hamish Macbeth hoarsely.

Hamish awoke late in the morning, feeling lazy and contented. He turned to gather Annie to him but found the other side of the bed empty. He got up and put on a dressing gown. Annie was in the kitchen, making coffee. She looked clean and fresh and was wearing her uniform. "We'd better get a move on," she said. "It's eleven o'clock already."

Hamish showered and dressed. He rumpled up the bed in the cell in the hope that Dick would think he had slept there.

Sleepy Dick was in the kitchen, grumbling that he had to have food and that a cup of coffee wasn't enough.

They piled into the Land Rover, Dick still

205

grumbling at having to share the back with Sonsie and Lugs. Hamish could only be glad that they had not created a fuss when he had shut them out of the bedroom.

He whistled happily as he drove over the heathery hills to Braikie. They had almost reached the boys' home when Annie's mobile rang. She answered it and Hamish heard her say, "Grand! See you tonight."

Her voice had been warm and affectionate. Hamish pulled up outside the boys' home and asked, "Who was that?"

"Oh, that was my husband," said Annie cheerfully. "He works on the oil rigs but he'll be home tonight."

"Dick," said Hamish stiffly, "would you mind getting out and letting me have a word in private?"

"Aye, sure," said Dick sadly.

Hamish turned to Annie. "Why didn't you tell me you were married?"

"Last night it didn't seem important," said Annie.

"So it wass chust a fling?"

"Don't look at me like that," said Annie hotly. "You enjoyed yourself, didn't you?"

"Women!" said Hamish savagely and banged his fist on the steering wheel.

Annie shrugged and got out.

After a few minutes, Hamish followed her.

■ ■ ■ ■

The boys had little to tell them that was any help at all. They had simply run away after finding the body.

"Now what?" asked Annie. "The Palfours?"

"It's Saturday," said Hamish. "Maybe you could have a word with the Palfour children, Annie. I'll drop you and Dick off. I'd like to get back to the station and go through all the alibis again. I'll pick you up later, Dick."

Hamish was studying his notes the next day when his phone rang. It was Annie. Hamish was still angry with her but he realised quickly that going on like the rejected lover was a waste of valuable time.

"I don't think this means anything," said Annie. "I was talking to Charles and Olivia in the garden. It was a bit creepy the way they seemed to be relishing this latest murder. Anyway, Fern Palfour came running down the garden, screaming that I had no right to speak to her children without an adult present. Charles grinned and said, 'Mummy's taken up dressmaking.' Fern turns the colour of mud and slaps him across the face. Then she burst into tears

207

and hugs him and apologises and then tells me to get the hell out of it. I don't think there's anything in it. What could be so awful about dressmaking?"

Hamish thanked her and rang off. He turned over what she had said in his mind but could not make any sense of it.

His phone rang again. "Hullo, boss," said a deep voice.

"Who is speaking?" demanded Hamish.

"Ginger Stuart. Listen, I've got something might interest you."

"Where are you?" asked Hamish sharply.

"At home."

"Stay there. Don't move. Don't open the door to anyone but me. Got it?"

"Sure, boss," said Ginger in a fake American accent.

Hamish rushed out to the Land Rover. The cat and dog scampered after him.

"No!" said Hamish. "Amuse yourselves for once!"

He raced off in the direction of Braikie.

Ginger opened the door to him. Even his tattoos seemed to be rippling with excitement.

Hamish followed him into a malodorous living room. The windows were open but he could smell pot.

"What have you got for me?" he asked.

"There was a broadcast this morning offering ten thousand pounds for any information leading to the murderers," said Ginger.

"Aye, and I'll see you get it if . . ."

"If I come up with the goods," said Ginger. "Here's what I picked up. I was in a bar on the road to Dingwall."

"Which one?"

"Marty's Mojo."

"Thieves' kitchen," commented Hamish, guessing that Ginger had probably gone there to buy drugs.

"Well, ye ken they have thae old-fashioned booths. There were these two blokes in the one the back o' me. I think they were a wee bittie stoned because they were giggling. But then one says to the ither, 'Maybe we should get out o' the country. I got friends in Spain.'

"The ither says, 'Spain's got an extradition treaty.'

" 'I hates foreigners,' says the ither. 'They'll never get back to us, Willy. We're safe as houses. We'll keep on lying low, don't spend the money until it's safe and then we can splash out a bit.'

"Then I heard one of them say, 'Thon was a rare rocket.' And his pal says, 'For Christ's sake, shut up.' What d'ye think o' that?"

Hamish's heart beat hard. "Who are these men?"

"I took a peek afore I left. Thin couple o' men wi' baseball caps pulled down over their eyes. I waited and waited and then I followed them home. It took me every effort to keep up. They was on a motorbike."

"Where did they go?"

"Here's the address," said Ginger triumphantly. "Twenty-four Southey's Lane, Dingwall."

"Thanks, I'll get on to it," said Hamish. "And yes, if this pans out, you'll get the award. By the way, cut out the pot smoking."

Outside, Hamish wondered whether to phone Jimmy and then decided against it. He would feel obliged to tell Blair, and Hamish didn't want the whole circus to descend on Dingwall and alert the two men. He called at the police station first and changed into civilian clothes. Then he hired an old Ford from the garage and set off.

The weather was crisp and clear. All thoughts of his night with Annie were lost in a sudden flood of hope and excitement.

Dingwall, perhaps the cleanest town in the Highlands, is blessed with many car parks. The town lies at the head of the Cromarty Firth. The name, *Dingwall,* means "parliament field" in Old Norse, showing the town was an important centre as far back as the arrival of the Vikings in AD 800.

Hamish walked down to the main street, went into the tourist office, and got a map of the town. Southey's Lane lay on the outskirts. He returned to the car park and drove off. Somehow he had expected to find a council estate, but Southey's Lane turned out to be a shabby row of cottages, bordering on ploughed fields.

He parked at the end of the row. Number 24 was in the middle.

Now what do I do? he wondered. If he confronted them, all they had to do was deny everything and then escape. He decided to wait and see if they came out. He fished out his camera and focused it.

An hour passed while he fretted. Then suddenly two men emerged. He shot off a photo. They got on a motorcycle and roared off. Hamish set off after them, cursing the old Ford's lack of speed. He could only hope they were going to Marty's Mojo as they disappeared in the distance.

Hamish heaved a sigh of relief when he saw the motorbike in the bar's car park. He phoned Jimmy and explained the situation. "Don't bring the whole lot," urged Hamish. "Just enough plainclothes to help me arrest them. Do you have to tell Blair?"

"No, he must have had a right bevy last night. The man was fair blootered. You've never seen a hangover like it. I'll get Dingwall police to back you up. Keep an eye on them and don't lose them. You should have told me immediately you had the news. I'll be over as fast as I can."

Hamish kept his eye on the entrance, worrying and fretting. Eventually a car drove into the car park, and four men in plain-clothes got out and approached Hamish. One flashed a warrant card and said, "Dingwall police."

"There are two men inside I want to arrest on suspicion of murder," said Hamish. "Take them back to the station. I'll show you who they are then I'll follow you and we'll wait for the contingent from Strathbane."

The two men, Terence Rattrey and Philip Windon, were driven from Dingwall police station to Strathbane. To Hamish's relief, Jimmy said he could sit in on the interviews the next morning.

They were an unsavoury-looking pair. Rattrey suited his name, being a rat-like man with beady eyes and a wispy brown moustache. Windon was pasty-faced, pimply, and sullen.

Despite long hours of questioning, all they could get out of the pair was "No comment" and a demand to see their lawyer.

At last, Daviot drew Jimmy and Hamish outside the interviewing room. "What do you think? I've a mind to let them have their lawyer. He might be able to talk some sense into them. We're digging up their backgrounds anyway. Hear this. Before they got into drugs, they were both in the Royal Engineers. They could have learned the knowledge to make that rocket and soup up the chair's engine in the forces."

"Who is this lawyer?" asked Hamish.

"William Lemont. Small time. Dingwall. Doesn't seem to have handled any criminal cases at all. He wasn't present when this pair were charged a few years ago with pushing drugs. They got out of jail last year."

"It's up to you," said Hamish, "but I feel uneasy about it, I don't know why."

"I'm going to phone him," said Daviot.

He went to his office and came back after ten minutes. "Lemont's on his way. Now all we can do is wait. Oh, Miss Williams, what is it?"

"The press have got wind of something and are massed outside, sir, and there's a minister from Dingwall wants to have a word with the men."

"What's his name?" asked Jimmy.

"Mr. Sutherland from the Church of St. Andrew."

"May as well let him see them. Maybe he can soften them up."

Hamish felt a qualm of unease. "I don't think anyone other than us should see them, sir."

"You've done enough here, Macbeth," said Daviot. "Get back to your station. We'll keep you informed." Daviot missed Blair, who was still off sick. Blair never contradicted or queried any of his ideas.

On the road back to Lochdubh, Hamish noticed that the tops of the mountains had their first covering of snow. He felt in his bones it was going to be a hard winter.

When he got back to the police station it was to find Matthew Campbell, editor of the *Highland Times,* waiting for him. "I thought I might get more out of you than I'd get out of Strathbane," he said. "What's happening?"

"I can only tell you that two men from Dingwall have been arrested on suspicion of murder," said Hamish. "You know I can't give you any more than that."

"Any little tidbit will do."

"Well, they're saying nothing until their lawyer arrives. A minister is visiting them."

"Which minister?"

"A Mr. Sutherland from St. Andrew's in Dingwall."

"That's odd," said Matthew.

"Why?"

"Sutherland is very old and creaky. Furthermore, he's an old intellectual. Hardly the type to want to console a couple of men suspected of murder. Besides, he's also not the sort to stir himself to arrive so quickly on the scene."

Hamish gave him an alarmed look. He darted into the office, ignoring Lugs who was banging his feed bowl on the floor, and seized the Highlands and Islands telephone directory. He phoned the reverend's number.

An old querulous voice answered the phone. "Mr. Sutherland," said Hamish, "we have had a report that you wish to see two prisoners accused of murder at Strathbane police headquarters."

"Now why would I do that? Who is speaking?"

"Sergeant Hamish Macbeth."

"With my arthritis, it is as much as I can do to get up into the pulpit on Sundays. Hullo!"

For Hamish had rung off.

He phoned Jimmy and howled, "Thon minister's a fake. Don't let him see the prisoners!"

"What's up, Hamish? The man's been and gone."

"And how are the prisoners?"

"Left them to sweat."

"That minister was an impostor. See that the prisoners are all right."

Jimmy seemed to be gone a long time. Hamish clutched the phone, hearing agitated voices shouting and yelling.

At last Jimmy came on telephone again, his voice hoarse with shock.

"They're dead, Hamish. Stone dead."

CHAPTER NINE

My barmie noddle's working prime.
— Robert Burns

Hamish returned to Strathbane in the morning. With the men dead, all hope of breaking the case had gone. Someone must have paid them to rig the stair lift, and that someone masqueraded as a minister to make sure they did not talk.

Hamish went straight to the detectives' room. "Anything on CCTV?" he asked Jimmy.

"You're never going to believe this," said Jimmy with a groan. "Look!"

Hamish leaned over him and studied the CCTV tape. The camera outside police headquarters swung from left to right. Whoever the murderer was, he had timed his entrance exactly for when the camera had swung away from the front door.

"And the CCTV that covers the car park?"

"Sprayed with black paint. He thought o' everything."

"What about the CCTV tapes from the surrounding streets?" asked Hamish.

"I'm just waiting for them to be collected."

"What are you doing here, Macbeth?" asked Blair, stomping up to them.

"Just making sure no evidence goes missing . . . again," said Hamish.

Blair backed off, muttering, "Aye, well, don't spend all day here."

"Where are the Palfours?" asked Hamish.

"The cleaners say they've gone back to Inverness for the day. We've sent someone to the auction rooms. I've heard they're selling off some of the old furniture. Inverness police are looking for them."

"Did no one think to search the minister?"

"It's Scotland. Ministers are God. No. He was carrying a Bible. He left it behind. The inside had been cut out and there were two empty miniatures of whisky in the cell. They died in agonies. Might be cyanide."

"Did no one hear their death throes?"

"There was a lot of crying and banging but instructions had been given to leave them alone to sweat it out. We seem to be dealing with a gang."

"Or someone with enough money to bribe

218

villains," said Hamish. "Any results from that cigarette end?"

"Too degraded to get anything."

Hamish waited patiently, drinking black coffee from cardboard cups until the CCTV tapes were delivered. Jimmy slotted them in and they both studied them.

"No one seems to be starving on the streets of Strathbane," murmured Hamish as one obese person after another lurched past on the screen.

"Shut up and let me concentrate," growled Jimmy.

"So what's the description of this fake minister?" asked Hamish. "What are we looking for?"

"He was tall with red hair, a fat face, and thick glasses."

"A disguise," said Hamish. "Pads in the cheeks and a wig."

"Probably."

"Hold it," said Hamish suddenly. "Freeze it right there."

"What do you see?"

"That boutique. Hilda's Fashions. Just going in the door. A tall black figure. It's black and white but that hair could be red. Can only see the back of him. I'm going round there."

■ ■ ■ ■

Hamish was met at the doorway of the boutique by Hilda Merrilee, a small, fussy woman.

"Thank goodness you came," she said. "I've never seen such a barefaced theft in my life."

"What happened?"

"This man came in . . ."

"Description?"

"Oh, let me see. Tall, soft-spoken, red hair and glasses."

"A dog collar?"

"He was wearing a scarf."

"So what exactly happened?"

"He said he was looking for a dress for his wife. He told me they were going to a wedding but that she was disabled and couldn't shop for herself. He said she was tall and quite plump. He looked at several gowns and then because we had a few customers, he asked if he could take them into a changing room and study them at his leisure. I showed him into a changing room. Then I had to go into another changing room to help a customer. After a time, I realised he hadn't come out. I went into the changing room. He had stolen one of our best gowns, a stole, and a big hat."

"What did the dress look like?"

"It was pale blue chiffon, long. The stole was paisley pattern, and the hat was a straw cartwheel with red silk rose on it."

"I'll get back to you," said Hamish. He rushed back to police headquarters where he told Jimmy what had happened and said, "Run the tapes again and look for a tall woman."

They sat together and studied the CCTV camera that showed the front of the shop.

"There!" exclaimed Hamish. It was a grainy picture of a tall figure, face hidden by a large straw hat, wearing a long dress and carrying a large carrier bag.

"See how loose the dress hangs," said Hamish. "He probably has his minister's clothes in the bag and the red wig. See if you can track him."

The figure disappeared into Barry's Superstore.

"Let's get round there," said Hamish.

In the security office at Barry's Superstore, Hamish studied the shop's security videos.

"Slow down," he ordered. "There he goes. Damn! As far as I remember, that's in the direction of the toilets, and they aren't covered."

He turned round and asked the security guard, "Is there a door at the back of the store?"

"A fire door."

"Is it locked?"

"No. Anyone can push down the bar and get out."

"Is the area outside covered by a camera?"

"No," said the guard. "Only the shop's rubbish out there."

"Come on," said Jimmy.

They hurried out through the store. The fire door was slightly open. They went outside. Rows of bins in a small area. Nothing else.

"I'll get some men round to go through the bins," said Jimmy. "He may have discarded the gown and we could get DNA from it."

"I think he'll have thought of that," said Hamish. "If I were him, I'd put everything in a bag weighted down with a brick and throw it into a peat bog. I think he had a car parked round here."

Jimmy glared at Hamish in frustration. "I think you should start checking the bins until I get some men round here."

"Yes, sir," said Hamish gloomily.

After Jimmy had gone, he half heartedly searched the bins, being pretty sure he

wouldn't find anything. When four policemen arrived, he left them to it.

He went back to police headquarters, hoping to have a look at some CCTV footage
of the streets around the store, but Jimmy
was now in a flaming temper and ordered
him back to Lochdubh.

Back at the police station, he was met by
the rumble of the dishwasher and the roar
of the television. He marched into his living
room where Annie and Dick were cosily
ensconced with cups of coffee.

"Switch that off!" he roared.

Dick hurriedly clicked off the television.
"Haven't you heard the latest?" demanded
Hamish.

"No," said Annie. "There seemed to be
nothing doing so we came back here."

Hamish told them what had happened.
"Now, I want both of you to help me think,"
he said. "If only the Palfours didn't have
such cast-iron alibis. They're the ones with
motive. They're the ones with enough
money to get people to do their dirty work."

"I've got some notes from a friend at the
Yard in London," said Annie, opening her
handbag and pulling out a sheaf of notes.
"Yes, Ralph Palfour was badly in debt. A
second mortgage was taken out on the

house in London. There is nothing but family pride to stop Palfour from selling the garden centre. A girl who used to work there said he had many offers to buy the place."

"Anyone in particular?"

"Estate agents. Oh, and some Russian oligarch who was interested in the place. Wanted to build a mansion."

"Name?"

"Let me see." She consulted her notes. "Ivan Andronovitch. Made his money in oil. I looked him up. No criminal record."

"There we have power and money," said Hamish. "He could have threatened the Palfours. What was this girl's impression of Palfour?"

"She said he was a good boss but weak and fussy. He was often heard saying that if his mother-in-law would just die, then all his troubles would be over."

"And did your friend at the Yard say they had found any sinister connection between Palfour and this Russian?"

"None whatsoever."

"I'd expect the press to be hammering at the door by now," said Dick.

"They're all over at Strathbane but some of them will be along here soon. I've got to think. I'm going out for a walk."

"I'd better get back to Strathbane," said Annie.

"If you hear anything interesting, let me know," said Hamish.

Annie left. Dick switched on the television again. Hamish glared at him, stuffed a sheet of notes in his pocket, and then called to the dog and cat and went out to the waterfront.

Hamish went into Patel's grocery store to buy himself a cup of coffee. Mr. Patel was unpacking bales of fabric.

"What's this?" asked Hamish. "A new line?"

"There's a dressmaking class at the village hall. A lot o' the women have decided to make their ain clothes," said Mr. Patel.

Hamish paid for a cup of coffee and went out and sat on a seat facing the loch. It was a grey misty day. The loch was like a sheet of metal. On the other side of the water, the forestry plantation looked ragged and denuded. There had been a decline in the Scottish timber business in recent years with many more tress being felled than were being planted. Critics believed that the environmental opposition to closely planted conifers had led to more emphasis on native woodland.

Two seals surfaced and swam along,

breaking the flat grey of the loch and sending out long ripples of waves on either side. He drank his coffee and stared into space.

"Dreaming, Hamish?" came Angela Brodie's voice from behind him. She walked round and sat down next to him.

Hamish told her of the latest development. "This is awful," said Angela. "I feel as if all the nastiness of the cities has come north to plague us."

Dressmaking, thought Hamish suddenly. Hadn't Charles Palfour said his mother had taken up dressmaking?

"What's this about a dressmaking class?" asked Hamish.

Angela looked surprised. "There's one tonight in the village hall, if you're interested. It's being run by the Currie sisters."

"Whit! Thon pair are an example of frump fashion."

"They just organise things. There's a Polish maid from the hotel who's a wizard."

"I might have a look at that," said Hamish. "What time?"

"Seven thirty. Planning on tailoring a new uniform?"

"You never know," said Hamish. "I'll maybe see you later. I've got to walk and think."

With Angela staring after him, he set off,

the dog and cat at his heels.

He walked all the way to the Tommel Castle Hotel, hoping suddenly to talk to Priscilla, only to find that she had left without even leaving a message for him.

He felt worried and depressed. Priscilla gone, Elspeth to get married, and all he had to show for a love life was a one-night stand with a married woman.

He scrounged a cup of coffee and took it to a quiet corner of the hotel lounge and began to study his notes, hoping against hope that he could find something he had previously missed.

What had Charles Palfour meant by that crack about dressmaking? Why had Fern Palfour been so alarmed that she had slapped him across the face? When Mary had been murdered, the Palfours had been staying in Inverness. They had been caught on a garage CCTV early the following morning as they made their way back to Braikie.

He decided to stay hidden for the rest of the day, out of the way of the press, and then visit the village hall. But he had forgotten that the press would need places to stay. Mr. Johnson came in to warn him, and Hamish and his pets escaped by the kitchen door.

He cut across the moors, not wanting to meet any of the press on the road. When he reached the back of the police station, he shoved up the kitchen window and climbed through. Sonsie and Lugs went round to the kitchen door and entered by the cat flap.

Hamish could hear the noise of the television from the living room. He sighed and began to make himself a fry-up and cook liver for the dog and cat. He was damned if he was going to cook anything for Dick.

But he should have known that Dick would not go hungry. Patel's sold mutton pies and when Hamish eventually went into the sitting room and switched off the television, he noticed that Dick had a tray in front of him bearing tea and the remains of two pies.

"Get your uniform on," ordered Hamish. "We're going to the village hall."

"Why?" asked Dick plaintively.

"Oh, chust dae as you're told," snapped Hamish. "You make your way out the front and say 'No comment' to the press and meet me at the village hall."

When Hamish and Dick entered the village hall, Mrs. Wellington, the minister's wife, approached them. "It's grand to see two gentleman being interested in dress-making," she said.

"Dick, here, is a transvestite," said Hamish maliciously.

"If you are here to make mischief, forget it," boomed Mrs. Wellington. "You may stay if you sit down quietly. She's about to begin."

A pretty Polish girl was standing at a long table with a pattern spread out on it.

"Now, ladies," she began, "I will first teach you how to follow a pattern."

She looked up as the door opened. The Currie sisters entered pushing an old-fashioned dressmaker's dummy on wheels in front of them, their faces red with exertion.

"This is the grand thing," said Nessie.

"Grand thing," echoed the Greek chorus that was her twin.

Hamish guessed the dummy was either Edwardian or Victorian. It had a bust like the figurehead on an old schooner and a wasp waist.

"It is so kind of you," said the Polish instructor diplomatically, "but I don't think any of us these days has a figure like that."

"You mean you can't use it?" demanded Nessie.

"Maybe we'll try later," she said.

Hamish stared at that dummy. His head started racing. The dummy was headless, but, he thought, put some sort of head on it and a wig and a hat, a coat and scarf say, put it in the front seat of a car, and it might show up on the CCTV as a real person. He got up abruptly and with Dick trotting after him returned to the police station.

"Go on," he said to Dick. "Watch your precious TV. I've got to think."

He went into the office and sat down. What if the two men had set up the chair lift, but it was Palfour who had lit the rocket? Somehow, the murder of Gloria was too violent and vicious for Ralph Palfour. And he certainly hadn't poisoned the prisoners.

But he could imagine a scenario where Mary knew something and tried to blackmail Palfour. How easy for Palfour to creep up behind her after arranging a meeting at the pool, strike her down, and then drown her.

He switched on his computer and began to trawl through the reports. The Palfours had said that on the night of Mary's murder, they had been staying at the Dancing Scotsman Hotel in Inverness. Hamish phoned the hotel and introduced himself to the manager.

"When Mr. and Mrs. Palfour were staying with you," he said, "was their room near a fire escape?"

"Wait a minute and I'll check," said the manager.

Hamish waited impatiently. At last the manager's voice came back on the phone.

"They were in room one hundred and sixty-three. It's at the end of the second-floor corridor. Yes, there is access to a fire escape."

Hamish thanked him and rang off. The dog and cat were fast asleep after their long walk. He went out to the Land Rover and drove to Strathbane.

Blair had fortunately gone home but Jimmy was still there, tired and rumpled and smelling of whisky. He tuned bloodshot eyes on Hamish and said, "What brings you?"

Hamish sat down and patiently began to outline everything he had found out, from Charles Palfour's remark about dressmaking to Scotland Yard's discovery of a connection to a Russian who wanted to buy the nursery, and then to the idea that Ralph Palfour could have sneaked out of the hotel to kill Mary, while his wife drove back the next morning with the dressmaker's dummy in the front seat made up to look like a man.

"Och, Hamish," said Jimmy wearily, "why on earth wouldn't Palfour then just drive back to Inverness and sneak back to his room? And how did he get to Braikie if he left the car with his wife?"

"I know, I know," said Hamish impatiently. "But who else has a motive for the murder? He's got a big people carrier. He could have stashed a motorbike in the back o' it. Get a search warrant for their house and their vehicle. See if there's a dressmaker's dummy in the house and get forensics to search the car to see if there's a trace of a motorbike."

"Hamish, hear this. Ye havenae a hope in hell. The Palfours have hired James Farquhar-Symondson. He's a Freemason. So is Daviot. So dear James is rumbling about police harassment and Daviot has told us to back off."

"You mean I can't do anything!"

Jimmy chewed his knuckles. Then he took a half bottle of Scotch out of his top drawer and took a slug.

"I've an idea," he said. "Look, it's the best I can come up with. You call on Palfour tomorrow as the sympathetic local bobby who just wants to know how they're getting on. Check with the maids. Ask them if they've seen a dummy anywhere."

"Right," said Hamish gloomily. "Meanwhile, I'd like to see the CCTV from that garage where they were supposed to be on the road back from Inverness."

Jimmy went away and then came back with a disk. "Help yourself."

Hamish studied the screen. The quality was not very good. There was Fern driving up. He froze the screen and focussed on the figure beside her. Baseball hat pulled down low and scarf over the lower part of the face. He sighed. It was impossible to tell whether it was a man or a dummy. He could only hope he could find out something the next day.

After checking his notes in the morning, he told Dick to try to speak to the maids at home as it was their day off. Dick was to ask them if they had seen a dressmaker's dummy anywhere in the house or had seen a motorbike.

He told Dick to use his own car, a battered old Honda, and set out leaving the dog and cat behind.

He was glad it was a weekday, which meant the children were in school. In a way, they unnerved him with their flat grey eyes and insolent faces.

The first thing he noticed was that the Palfours had a new car, a large BMW. What had happened to the people carrier?

Hamish rang the bell. After what seemed

a long time, Ralph Palfour opened the door. "This is police harassment," he shouted. "I'm calling my lawyer."

Hamish put a vacant expression on his face and said mildly, "Och, it iss nothing but the neighbourly visit. I chust wanted to see you were all right and that the press havenae been bothering you, sir."

Palfour visibly relaxed. "They were all round yesterday but our lawyer dealt with them."

"Thon's a grand car," said Hamish, grinning foolishly. "What happened to your old one?"

"I sold it."

"Who to?"

"A garage over in Dingwall."

"All the way there?" marvelled Hamish. "Now which garage would that be?"

"Ferry's Motors. Look, I have things to do so shove off!"

He went in and slammed the door in Hamish's face.

Hamish drove as far as the car park in the glen. It was deserted. A cold wind was blowing from the north, sending discarded rubbish running across the gravel of the park. The half-finished gift shop looked bleak.

234

Police tape fenced off the entrance to the glen.

He took out his phone, got the number of Ferry's Motors, and dialled. He asked to speak to the manager. After introducing himself, he said, "I believe a Mr. Ralph Palfour sold his Peugeot people carrier to you."

"Yes, that's right."

"When was that?"

"That would be on the twelfth."

Two days after Mary's murder, thought Hamish. "Could you give me the address of the customer who bought it?"

"Hold on."

Hamish waited. The wind rustled through the coloured leaves of the autumn trees in the glen, making a whispering sound. Hamish had an uneasy feeling of being watched.

At last the manager's voice came back on the phone. "The buyer was a Mr. James Petrie of The Loans, Glebe Street, Cnothan."

Hamish thanked him and rang off, relieved he would not have to go all the way to Dingwall. Cnothan was on his beat.

As he drove in the direction of Cnothan, the wind had risen and was buffeting the car. He was driving through an expanse of moorland where a winding river already had angry little waves speeding across its surface.

When he reached the village of Cnothan, he noticed angrily that double yellow lines had been painted down both sides of the main street to prevent parking. Why? he wondered. Why try to take away trade from the shops?

He noticed a few cars were nonetheless parked in the main street, but he had no intention of ticketing anyone.

Glebe Street, he remembered, was a narrow lane parallel to the road running alongside the loch.

The Loans was a sandstone villa, Scottish Georgian from the look of it, and Hamish guessed it had once been a manse.

He parked in the short drive, got out, and rang the bell. A haggard blonde woman answered the door. She was wearing a red sweater and jeans so tight they looked as if they had been pasted onto her thin, middle-aged figure.

As soon as she saw Hamish, she said, "And about time!"

"You mean you were expecting a visit from the police?"

"Of course. You've come about our stolen car, haven't you?"

Hamish's heart sank. He removed his cap.

"May I come in? This is verra important."

She stood back to let him past and then ushered him into a soulless living room. A mushroom-coloured three-piece suite decorated with gold fringe stood on a mushroom-coloured fitted carpet. Two nests of tables were on either side of the sofa.

A huge flat-screen TV dominated one wall and steel-framed pictures of angry-looking abstracts were hung on the others.

"My work," said Mrs. Petrie proudly, waving a hand with long French nails at the paintings.

"Very fine," said Hamish. "Now, about our car."

"It happened last night. We were having our dinner and the TV was on."

"In here?" asked Hamish.

"Yes, those tables. We didn't hear a thing. James went to put the cat out and found he was looking at an empty space where the new car had been. We reported the loss to the police."

"Did you tell them that the previous owner had been a Mr. Palfour?"

"No. Why? Oh! You mean that man whose mother-in-law was murdered?"

"The same."

"Are we in danger?"

"I shouldn't think so. I'll get on it right

away. Where is your husband?"

"He was late for work because he did not get the courtesy car delivered from the insurance company until ten this morning. His company is along the waterfront. It's called Shopmark Fashions. It's doing grand. He got a good grant from the Highlands and Islands Board because we employ a lot of the local people."

"I'll be off then."

As she walked him to the door, she hooked an arm through his and smiled up at him. Hamish marvelled that any woman could be bothered sticking on false eyelashes so early in the day. "Call anytime," she murmured huskily, giving his arm a squeeze.

"Aye, right," said Hamish, gently disengaging himself.

As he drove off, he felt a stab of pity for her. What a life, stuck in a grim highland village like Cnothan with winter on the threshold. All dressed up and nowhere to go.

He drove to the factory and was soon ensconced in James Petrie's office. Mr. Petrie was a small, round, florid man. He could only repeat what his wife had said. "My car's probably on its way to Bulgaria now," he complained.

When Hamish left him, he phoned Dick.

"Neither o' the maids has seen anything like a dressmaker's dummy in the house," said Dick. "And they havenae seen a motorbike, either."

Hamish then phoned Jimmy. "Damn!" said Jimmy. "Maybe I'll see if I can get a forensic team over to the Petries' house. I've got the registration number of the Palfours' old car and I'll put out an alert. We're being blocked at every turn, Hamish. Get back to Ferry's Motors and see if Palfour tried to sell a motorbike as well. If you've no luck there, phone all the motor sales places you can think of."

Hamish spent the rest of the day on the phone without success. He went out to shut his hens up for the night and check on his sheep when he noticed a saucer of milk outside the kitchen door. He went back inside, where Dick was once more in front of the television. Hamish switched it off. "Did you put that milk outside the door?"

"Well, yes, but . . ."

"The cat is not allowed milk. It gives her diarrhea."

"It's no' for the cat." Dick's face turned red.

Hamish looked at him in amazement. "Neffer tell me it's for the fairies!"

239

"You see," said Dick, "there just may be something in it. Better be safe. I thought you needed some help."

"Of all the superstitious twaddle . . ."

Hamish stomped off to do his chores. The wind buffeted him on his way back to the police station.

The saucer of milk was empty. "Hedgehog," muttered Hamish.

Beyond the shelter of the side of the police station, the wind screeched down the loch. Better get the candles out, thought Hamish. There's bound to be a power cut if this storm goes on.

The phone was ringing when he went in. He rushed to answer it. It was Nessie Currie. "Can you help me, Hamish?" she asked.

"What's up?"

"It's our dressmaker's dummy. Mrs. Palfour lent it to us the other day but nobody wants to use it. She's just phoned and wants it back but it won't fit in our little car and . . ."

"Don't touch it!" shouted Hamish. "I'll be right along."

CHAPTER TEN

By fairy hands their knell is rung,
By forms unseen their dirge is sung.
— Wilkie Collins

"Why are you so interested in our dummy?"
asked Nessie. "Is it your feminine side? I
read this article . . ."

"No," said Hamish. "I must take it with
me."

"It's in the front room."

Hamish went into the front room carrying
a roll of plastic and tape. He proceeded to
carefully cover it up and seal it.

Then he dug out a receipt, filled it in, and
gave it to Nessie. "Thanks," he said.

"But what do you want it for?" wailed
Nessie.

"I'll let you know," said Hamish, trundling
the dummy on its wheels out of the door.

Jessie came in and said to her sister, "Was

241

that Hamish?"

"Aye, the man's mad keen to get that dummy."

"He's not married," said Jessie with a sly look at her sister.

"Do you think he's homosexual?"

"Maybe. I mean a man his age and not wed."

They settled down to a delicious and scurrilous gossip.

Hamish phoned Jimmy with the news then set off to Strathbane. An excited Jimmy was outside police headquarters, waiting for him.

"Don't bring it out," he said, when Hamish arrived. "Take it straight to the lab. "We're getting an expert up from Glasgow to enhance that garage CCTV. Daviot's right pleased with you."

"I noticed it had been sawn and then glued together again. They'd need to have done that to reduce the size and to make it look like a man."

The Currie sisters' phone rang as Hamish Macbeth was driving back to Lochdubh.

Fern Palfour's voice came on the line. "Miss Currie," she said, "I thought you were going to bring that dressmaker's dummy back to me."

"I was that," said Nessie. "I asked Hamish Macbeth for help with it because it's too big to get in our wee car and he . . . Hullo! Hullo!

"She's rung off," said Nessie to her sister. "Some folks! But that's the English for you."

At Strathbane the next morning, Hamish found to his disappointment that the CCTV images couldn't be enhanced enough to give any proof that it was a dummy and not a man in the car sitting next to Fern Palfour. The lab, however, reported that both Fern and Ralph Palfour's fingerprints were on the dummy. There were also traces of glue at the neck showing where something could have been stuck on.

"Where's Jimmy?" Hamish asked Annie Williams.

"He's gone with Blair to pull the Palfours in for questioning."

Hamish felt uneasy. They could of course say that it was natural that their fingerprints were on it as they had both carried it to the car when they were delivering it to the Currie sisters.

Daviot would eventually cave in and let them have their high-powered lawyer and that would be that.

And that was that, as Jimmy confirmed later. "Nothing to hold them on," he said gloomily. "Thon pair were the height of hurt and furious respectability. Daviot let them have their lawyer in and everything was over bar Blair's shouting."

When he had rung off, Hamish went into his living room, prised the remote control from Dick's fingers, and switched off the television.

"Dick, when you questioned the maids about that dummy, are you sure they said it was nowhere in the house? What about the attics?"

"They said that they were asked when they started the job to clean the place from top to bottom, attics and all."

Hamish went into the police office and sat down and stared into space.

If it wasn't anywhere in the house, he suddenly thought, maybe they bought it. But where? Then he remembered the auction rooms in Inverness.

He phoned up and asked to speak to Mr. Simon, one of the auctioneers. "Do you remember selling an old-fashioned tailor's dummy?" he asked.

"I'll need to check the records. Can you wait?"

Hamish waited impatiently. The man

244

seemed to be gone a long time. Then he came back on the line and said, "Yes, it was sold with a lot of junk a few days ago."

"Who bought it?"

"A Mr. Hamish Macbeth. Was that you?"

"No, it wasn't. What address?"

"The police station, Lochdubh. That *is* you."

"No it's not, I can assure you. Do you have CCTV in the auction room?"

"Yes."

"Do you still have the old disks?"

"Yes, we keep them for three months."

"I'll be down there as soon as I can," said Hamish.

Hamish set off with the siren wailing and the blue light flashing, breaking the speed limit to Inverness. He collected the CCTV disk which covered the day of the sale of the dummy and then headed full speed to Strathbane after phoning Jimmy.

"I hope you've got something," grumbled Jimmy. "Let's have a look."

He slotted the disk into the computer. "Go forward to the tenth September at eleven in the morning," urged Hamish.

"Here we are. No sound but, by all that's holy, there's the dummy on top of a box of stuff."

The camera panned over the auction room. "There!" said Hamish. "Freeze it!"

At the back of the auction room, his catalogue raised to place a bid, was Ralph Palfour.

"Gotcha!" shouted Jimmy.

Blair suddenly appeared. "Whit's going on?"

Jimmy told him.

"Take some men and bring them in," said Blair. "Take Annie Williams with you in case the children are there. I want her tae stay wi' them. Right?"

"Right, sir," said Jimmy. "Aren't you coming, sir?"

"No, I'll just tell Mr. Daviot."

When Hamish and Jimmy had left, Blair went outside to the car park. If this proved to be successful, then all the kudos would go to Hamish Macbeth and he felt he couldn't bear that. He phoned Ralph Palfour from a public phone box and said, "Just to let you know, Mr. Palfour, that I have sent men to arrest you. We have proof that the dummy was bought by you at the auction house in Inverness."

Then he rang off.

Hamish Macbeth was puzzled as he drove back to Lochdubh. He was sure that they

246

were on the edge of solving the murders, and yet he felt uneasy. The Palfours should have burned that dummy. Their arrogance in thinking they could get rid of it by giving it to the Currie sisters was nearly beyond belief. But Hamish knew from experience that villains were always arrogant. That probably explained why Ralph Palfour had been stupid enough to use a policeman's name in the auction room.

He stopped off in the village to buy groceries.

When he returned to the police station, the phone was ringing. Dick had the sound on the television up so high, he did not hear it. Hamish ran into the office and answered it. It was Jimmy, his voice high and angry with frustration.

"They've gone, Hamish, the kids as well."

"They may just be out for the day."

"Mrs. McColl, the maid, said they packed up a lot of stuff including the remaining stuff they hadn't already sold from the strong room and took off. They said they were going abroad on holiday. We're checking their bank accounts. We hope to put a freeze on them but they may have got there before us. There are no CCTV cameras north o' Strathbane. They could be anywhere. We've set up roadblocks."

"Scotland Yard should be keeping an eye on the movements of that Russian," said Hamish. "Jimmy, it was unlike Blair not to want to be with you."

"What are you saying?"

"What if the auld scunner tipped them off?"

"Och, come on, Hamish. He can be daft at times but not that daft. I'll keep you posted."

A week went by. The Palfours seem to have disappeared into thin air. If this Russian were behind the whole thing, thought Hamish gloomily, they might even be dead.

A hard frost settled on the Highlands. It was so cold that slivers of ice began to appear along the shore of the sea loch. The Fairy Glen was deserted. White trees with a few remaining leaves studied their reflections in the pool.

The mountains loomed up against a pale blue sky. Smoke from peat fires rose straight up into the air from cottage chimneys.

During the week, Hamish had questioned as many people as he could in Braikie, hoping someone might have seen the Palfours, but without success.

He was awakened on Saturday morning with a ferocious banging at the door and

Archie Maclean, the fisherman, shouting, "There's a woman drowning in the loch, Hamish! I'll get the boat out."

Something made Hamish pause to strap his skean dhu on his ankle. He was afterwards to put it down to a sixth sense of fear.

In his vest and underpants, he ran out of the police station, vaulted over the seawall, and waded into the icy waters of the loch, gasping at the cold as he swam out to where a figure was struggling. As he swam near, he recognised the features of Fern Palfour. He had almost reached her when he was seized by the ankles and dragged down into the icy black depths.

A black figure with a light on its head and scuba diving equipment was below him. He drew his dagger and sliced the air pipe, feeling his ankles released. He gave the figure as hard a kick on the head as he could manage.

He shot to the surface, dropping the skean dhu to the bottom of the loch, then swam to Fern, grabbed her, and began to pull her to the shore. Villagers were waiting with blankets. Fern was a deathly colour. Hamish crouched down by Fern, performing every lifesaving technique he could remember, until water gushed from her mouth. She recovered consciousness for a moment and whispered "They made me" before relapsing.

"An ambulance is coming," said Mrs. Wellington. "Here's Dr. Brodie."

"Help me get her along to the surgery," said Dr. Brodie, "and send the ambulance there. Hamish, you come, too. It's a wonder you aren't dead."

"There's a man in the loch, a scuba diver, who tried to pull me down," said Hamish. "Get a boat out to Archie and tell him to search around. I'll need to phone Strathbane."

He returned to the police station, wrapped in blankets. His teeth were beginning to chatter as the adrenaline that had fuelled his rescue began to ebb.

"I've run you a hot bath," said Dick. "Get in it and I'll bring you some tea."

"Got to phone first."

"I've done that," said Dick. "Off you go. I'll put two hot-water bottles in your bed."

Hamish did not go to bed. Relieved to find he had stopped shivering, meaning that any hypothermia he was suffering must be mild, Hamish dressed in a flannel shirt and sweater and his thickest trousers, socks, and boots. He took the two hot-water bottles out of the bed and clutched them to him.

"I've made you a glass of toddy," fussed Dick. "Nothing like whisky, sugar, and lemon wi' a wee drop o' water to get you on your feet again. Then you havenae had any breakfast. A plate of porridge is what you need."

"Yes, Daddy," said Hamish. "I'm right grateful. But before that, could you go outside and see if they've got that diver? I'm still feeling a bit cold, and I don't want to go outside yet."

After a long while, Dick came back with Jimmy. Hamish explained what had happened.

"I'm waiting for the police divers," said Jimmy. "How did you manage to escape?"

"I kicked him," said Hamish. He knew that any mention of the dagger would lead to endless paperwork and endless enquiries. Blair would try to get him accused of culpable homicide.

"He could have got out of the loch on the other side and made his way off through the forestry," said Dick.

"Fern said, 'They made me do it,' " said Hamish. "How is she?"

"By the time she got to the hospital, she was hanging on by a thread. The way I look at it," said Jimmy, "whoever 'they' are, they forced her into that loch. Somehow, they blame you for the whole thing coming apart. We'll need to hope she recovers. When you're feeling better, send over your report."

The dead body of the diver was caught in a strong current as the tide went out, and pulled out to sea. When the tide turned, the body was carried towards the cliffs at the entrance to the loch. There giant waves hammered it time and again against the cliffs and jagged rocks, before turning again and dragging the remains back out to sea.

Fern Palfour died in hospital without saying another word. Britain from the north to the south was scoured for the missing Palfours, but without success. For a week, the press besieged the police station in Lochdubh before finally giving up. Hamish had been ordered by Daviot to stay indoors and not to speak to them.

The Sutherland weather performed one of its changes as the wind moved round to the west and brought mild weather.

It was sheer desperation that prompted Hamish Macbeth to pay a visit on the seer Angus Macdonald. He did not believe in Angus's second sight, but knew he had a vast fund of knowledge of the area.

He bought a packet of good coffee from Patel's and set off up the brae to the seer's, rubbing repellent on his face and neck, for the milder weather had brought the midges out again. He marvelled at their survival, wondering how the hard frost hadn't killed them off.

"What brings ye, Hamish?" said Angus, opening the door to him and then ushering him in.

"You're the seer. You're supposed to know," said Hamish, sitting down in a chair by the peat fire where a blackened kettle on a chain hung over the flames. Angus had a perfectly good electric kettle in the kitchen, but he liked to create an old-fashioned atmosphere for visitors.

"Stop joking and tell me," said Angus, lowering himself into a battered armchair opposite and stroking his long grey beard.

Hamish handed him the packet of coffee, which Angus took with an appreciative grunt.

"It's like this," said Hamish. "We've searched high and low for the missing Palfours. You've a grand knowledge of the county. Can you think of any old building or ruin we might not have searched?"

Angus sat for a long time in silence while the rising wind howled around the old cottage like a banshee.

Then he closed his eyes. At last he said in a low crooning voice, "Between here and Lairg there's a ruined cottage. Belonged a long time ago to a shepherd. It has a cellar."

"Where precisely is this cottage?" demanded Hamish.

Angus opened his eyes. "I cannae see any mair."

"It's a damn long way between here and Lairg," snapped Hamish. "Och, you're a waste o' time."

He got up to leave.

"Go carefully," said Angus. "Death is stalking ye."

Hamish stood for a moment by the doorway, suddenly uneasy. Then he shrugged and left.

"Old fraud," he muttered angrily as he set off down the brae. On the other hand, he thought wearily, I've nothing else.

At the police station, to his surprise, lazy Dick offered to go with him. "Nothing on television?" asked Hamish.

"Truth is, I'm right sick o' television," said Dick.

With Sonsie and Lugs in the back of the Land Rover, they set off. Hamish drove steadily and slowly, looking to right and left.

They reached a stretch of road where the pillared mountains rose on one side; there was moorland on the other, with the River Oykel winding through it.

"Stop!" cried Dick suddenly.

Hamish screeched to a halt. Lugs barked and Sonsie hissed with alarm. "Over there," said Dick, "by that stand o' trees."

Hamish's eyes followed his pointing finger. "Och, Dick, thon is too much o' a ruin."

"But you said you were looking for a cellar," protested Dick.

"What would a shepherd be doing with a cellar?" grumbled Hamish. "Oh, well, come on. May as well have a look."

The wind was hissing through the heather as they walked towards the ruin with Sonsie and Lugs scampering after them.

The building was roofless, and the back wall and one on the right-hand side had disappeared. Locals at one time had probably come to take away the slates and stones for another building, thought Hamish.

"Nothing here," said Dick. "This place fair gies me the creeps. Let's go."

"Wait!" urged Hamish. He took a torch from his belt and shone it on a pile of stones, then on the floor. "These stones have been moved recently," he said. "Help me move them." The old cottage had been built from stones, hammered into shape.

With Dick mumbling and cursing, they carried stone after stone to one side.

"There's a door," exclaimed Dick. "It looks new."

They heaved the last of the stones away. There was a key in the lock. Hamish turned it, and the door swung open on well-oiled hinges. A short flight of crumbling steps led down to a cellar.

Hamish, shining his torch, made his way down.

Three bodies lay trussed up on the floor — Ralph Palfour and the children. Olivia and Charles had rolled together for warmth. Hamish felt Ralph Palfour's neck and wrist for a pulse. "He's dead," he said bitterly. He then inspected Olivia and got a faint pulse; the same with Charles. He cut the ropes that bound them.

"We might be able to save these two," he said urgently. "I'll phone for police and ambulance. You'll find rugs, a flask of brandy, and my rifle in the back. Bring all the stuff here."

"You shoudnae be carrying a weapon without permission."

"I don't give a toss," howled Hamish. "Get it. I don't want to be here unarmed in case they come back."

When Dick returned, he wrapped the children in rugs and tried to force a little brandy between their lips.

"I think I'm losing them," he said. "Will that ambulance never arrive?"

Then, to his relief, he heard the sound of a helicopter overhead and Dick outside, shouting and yelling.

Hamish stuffed his rifle down his trouser leg and waited anxiously, letting out a sigh of relief as two men from Mountain Rescue clattered down the stairs with a stretcher.

A police helicopter then arrived with Jimmy, three police officers, and Annie Williams.

"Annie had better go to the hospital with the children," said Hamish.

"Is Palfour dead?"

"Yes. I think it was cold and starvation. I don't know how those children managed to survive. Where's Blair?"

"Day off. Scenes of crimes'll be here soon. Is that a flask?"

"Aye."

"Gimme a slug. Let's get outside or we'll be accused of compromising a crime scene."

Hamish made his way awkwardly up the stairs. "What's up with your leg?" asked Jimmy.

"I think I injured it in the loch," said

Hamish, hoping to get rid of Jimmy so he could get the rifle out of his trouser leg.

Outside, Jimmy said, "How on earth did you find this godforsaken place?"

"The seer, Angus Macdonald, must know every house, ruined or otherwise, in Sutherland."

"Good work, Hamish. Get your full report in."

"If it's all right with you, I'd like to get to the hospital in the hope the children stay alive."

"All right."

"Which hospital?"

"Strathbane."

Watched suspiciously by Jimmy, Hamish limped towards the Land Rover. He went around the side where he was sheltered from Jimmy's view, took out the rifle, and put it beside Dick in the passenger seat. Then he whistled for his pets and got them in the back.

"We'll drop this rifle off at the station," said Hamish, "and then we'll get to the hospital in Strathbane."

The Palfour children were suffering from malnutrition and hypothermia. They were both in a private room in hospital with tubes attached to them.

Hamish sat on a bench outside with Annie Williams. They were told that if the siblings showed good signs of recovery, then they could try to speak to them. Blair joined them, fell asleep, woke up after an hour, and said he was going home but would be back in the morning.

Hamish felt obscurely relieved that Annie's company did not trouble him in any way. He felt that if the Palfour children talked to anyone, they would talk to her.

Two policemen were on guard outside their room. They had orders to supervise any member of the medical staff who entered the room in case someone decided to masquerade as a doctor and silence the children.

At two in the morning, Hamish and Annie had fallen asleep when the fire alarm went off.

Hamish and Annie awoke. There was a smell of smoke in the air. Two hospital porters and a nurse went into the children's room.

Hamish followed by Annie rushed in after them. "Get out o' here!" roared Hamish. "I think it's a trick. Leave them!"

The two policemen on guard followed him in. "Shut the door," ordered Hamish, "and all of us into the bathroom. There's no smoke in here."

They crowded into the adjoining bath-room. Hamish left the door open a crack.

"I hope you're right," muttered Annie. "We might all go up in flames."

"We'll go down in flames if anything happens to them," said Hamish.

He applied his eye to the crack in the door. A figure in a white coat entered, looked around, and approached the bed.

Hamish darted out and seized the man. He fought furiously until he was overwhelmed by Hamish, Annie, and the two police guards.

He was a tall man with glasses. Hamish clipped the handcuffs on him, read him his rights, charging him with attempted murder after finding a syringe in his pocket.

All the prisoner would say was, "No comment." Hamish phoned police headquarters and waited until a tired and rumpled Jimmy arrived with other detectives to take the man into custody.

"I think you might find he was the one who poisoned those two prisoners," said Hamish.

The fire had been a false alarm. Someone had set fire to a bundle of newspapers in a wastepaper bucket at the end of the corridor.

Hamish and Annie continued their vigil, both finally falling asleep again, not waking until eight in the morning.

Dick appeared, bearing a tray with cardboard containers of coffee and two bacon rolls. "Thought you might be hungry," he said. "I brought you an electric razor as well."

"I'll go and wash and shave after I've drunk this coffee," said Hamish. "Come and get me if it looks as if either of the children is awake."

He had just finished shaving when Dick put his head round the door and said, "They're awake. The doctor says we can have a quick word."

Hamish hurried back. Annie was already in the hospital room, sitting between the beds, holding a tape recorder.

"What happened?" Annie was asking gently.

Olivia replied in a faint voice. "Mum said we were moving to a new house and we had to hurry. I don't know where we were when we were forced off the road. They took us to that cellar and tied us up and left us. They were speaking some foreign language but then I heard one say in English, 'Leave them to rot.' We all shouted and shouted until we were too weak to shout any more." She began to cry.

"That's quite enough for now," said a doctor who had been supervising the interview. He hustled them out of the room.

Outside, he said, "They had better be left in peace for the rest of the day. I would like a psychiatrist to see them. The poor lambs have to be told at some point that both their parents are dead."

Hamish and Annie were joined at that point by Blair and Jimmy. Blair was furious. The prisoner who had tried to kill the children was refusing to talk despite a long night of questioning. But they had taken his fingerprints, said Jimmy, and he was a John Witherspoon from Dingwall with a long list of previous convictions for drug dealing. The syringe contained a massive dose of thallium.

Blair stumped off. Jimmy said, "There's a posse from MI6 flying up. Blair's desperate to take the credit."

"Let him," said Hamish who had a fear of being promoted and forced out of his police station. He often wondered how long he could stay on in Lochdubh. Proposals were afoot to close police stations from Beauly to

Betty Hill.

"What now?" asked Annie when Jimmy had left.

"I think we should get some sleep," said Hamish. "There's nothing more we can do today."

CHAPTER ELEVEN

Mammon led them on,
Mammon, the least erected spirit that fell
From heaven, for even in heaven his
   looks and thoughts
Were always downward bent, admiring
   more
The riches of heaven's pavement,
   trodden gold,
Than aught divine or holy else enjoyed
In vision beatific

                    — John Milton

Hamish was awakened in the early afternoon by Dick shaking him. "Jimmy wants us over in Strathbane," he said. "Witherspoon's cracked."

Hamish hurriedly washed and dressed and put on his uniform. He told the dog and cat to stay and set off for Strathbane, pushing his way through a throng of excited press to get into headquarters.

Jimmy met him in the detectives' room and said, "Take a seat and read the bastard's statement."

"I'm hungry," said Dick plaintively. "I'll go to the canteen and get us something."

Hamish settled down and began to read with growing horror. Ivan Andronovitch had wanted the land the nursery was on to build a mansion. He learned that Ralph Palfour was heavily in debt and began to cultivate him. Ralph confided that he would be rich if only his mother-in-law would die.

The Russian had contacted Witherspoon, who was in charge of drug distribution in the north for him, and told him to hire a couple of villains to arrange a colourful death for Mrs. Colchester. He wanted to keep Palfour frightened.

Witherspoon had hired Terence Rattrey and Philip Windon, knowing they would do anything for drugs. Rattrey had been an electrical engineer but, because of his drug taking, had lost jobs. Windon was the one who had crept into the hunting box, super-glued the safety belt, and then lit the rocket that had sent Mrs. Colchester to her death. Mrs. Colchester had sat like a stone, staring into the shadowy hall, and did not see him. Rattrey had been waiting on the top landing, ready to pour nail varnish remover over the banisters.

Then Gloria McQueen had phoned Ralph Palfour and said that she had seen two men over at a quarry near Drim. She thought they were playing with fireworks. Now she was beginning to wonder if it had anything to do with him.

Ralph had been given Witherspoon's phone number in case of emergency. He phoned him right way. Windon and Rattrey were promised fifty thousand pounds to get rid of Gloria fast. They were in Braikie at that time, enjoying the fact that no one suspected them. They had found Gloria in her garden with the chain saw and had killed her. They had been wearing workmen's overalls and had shed them because they were blood-spattered, dumping them in a peat bog.

Then Witherspoon learned they had been arrested. He knew they had to die and so masqueraded as a minister.

He insisted he wasn't in on the Palfours' abduction.

"He says nothing about the murder of Mary Leinster," said Hamish.

"He swears blind he had nothing to do with that. My guess is that she knew something and that Ralph met her in the glen and got rid of her himself."

266

"Anyway, there's something to be said for Blair at last," said Hamish. "He got him to crack."

"Oh, that wasnae Blair. It was the bods from MI6."

"I'm going back to the hospital," said Hamish. "I want to see if that psychiatrist got anything out of Olivia and Charles."

The psychiatrist, a Dr. Filey, agreed to see Hamish. He was an elderly man with a shock of white hair and a clever face, crisscrossed with wrinkles.

"Did the children speak to you?" asked Hamish.

"Yes, they did."

"Did you tell them of their parents' death?"

"I did. I'm not usually shocked, but that pair startled me. Olivia asked if that meant she and Charles would inherit the money. I said I did not know, it was a matter for the courts — but people could not benefit from a crime, so the money would probably go to the state. Charles cursed me. He then said his parents were a couple of weak losers. After that, they clammed up and wouldn't speak to me."

"What will happen to them?"

"If we can't find any living relatives, they'll

be fostered. I have an awful feeling they are a pair of psychopaths. They didn't even want to know how their mother had died. However, they want to stay in the north."

Hamish met Jimmy coming out of the children's room. He was followed by Annie Williams. "No go," he said. "They just look at us with blank eyes and then tell us to get lost. The doctor's in there with them. He told us they were badly traumatised and to leave them alone."

"Did the Palfours draw out any money before they fled?"

"Aye, five hundred thousand. The Russian crooks have probably got it. Thanks to Witherspoon, we've begun to round up every drug dealer in the Highlands. But Andronovitch has fled the country."

"I wish I could get my hands on that Russian," raged Hamish. "All those dead people! He's probably got enough money salted away to keep him in comfort for the rest of his life."

"We'll just need to be pragmatic," said Jimmy. "The monster's head has been cut off so all the little monsters are under arrest. The Highlands will be clear o' drugs for a bit."

"Until the next monster arrives," said Hamish.

■ ■ ■ ■

Ivan Andronovitch was in his fastness in the Ukraine, surrounded by guards. He sat in his office, going through facts his minions had gathered on every policeman in the Palfour case. One name kept sticking out. Hamish Macbeth. He found it hard to believe that a village policeman should have brought about his downfall, and he thirsted for revenge. He had arranged for Fern Palfour to fake drowning in the hope of getting rid of Macbeth. Although he hadn't quite believed it at the time, he had been told that Macbeth was the most dangerous one. He sighed. "If you want a job done properly," he said to the uncaring walls of his office, "do it yourself."

A month went by, a month in which Hamish still felt uneasy. The Highlands had settled down into their usual torpor. Press and tourists had gone and the only excitement in Lochdubh was the visit of a hellfire minister to take over while Mr. Wellington was recovering from swine flu. The villagers loved a short exposure to hell and damnation.

Hamish called one day at Braikie Academy

to see how the Palfour children were settling down. The headmaster, a rubicund Welshman called Parry Jones, assured Hamish that they were adjusting very well.

"Have they any friends?" asked Hamish.

"I'm not sure. But the school counsellor, Jane Anstruther, has been seeing them. I'll phone her and see if she's free."

Ten minutes later, Hamish was sitting in Jane's office, sipping an excellent cup of coffee. Jane Anstruther was in her early thirties with a round rosy face and curly brown hair.

"I don't think either Olivia or Charles has any friends . . . yet. It's still early days."

"The psychiatrist who saw them when they were in hospital said he was afraid they were a couple of psychopaths."

"I find that shocking," she said angrily. "I know he has a good reputation, but to make such a judgement after all they had been through!"

"I think he was shocked that they did not grieve for their parents or ask what had happened to their mother. They were only concerned to know if they could still inherit."

"I still find that understandable. The dramatic loss of both parents would leave them bereft and wondering what was to become of them. I gather, from reports, that the whole tragedy was set in motion by Ralph Palfour's desire for money. He must have given his children an idea that only money was important. They are quiet and obedient and anxious to settle down. They have good foster parents, Jeannie and Hugh Mallard. They report that the children are no trouble at all. They still board at the school during the week and stay with the Mallards at the weekends."

"Have they been bullying any of the other children? Demanding money?"

"Really, Mr. Macbeth, I am beginning to get very angry with you. Here are two innocent lambs, doing their best to come to terms with normal life. I don't want you near them. In fact, I am going to complain to your superiors about your attitude. Now, goodbye!"

Hamish decided he had better visit the Mallards right away before any orders came down from above to stop him doing so.

The Mallards had a tidy bungalow in a new housing estate in Braikie. Their bungalow was called Samarkand. Hamish rang the doorbell, which chimed out a short burst of "Scotland the Brave."

The door was opened by a faded elderly woman wearing an old-fashioned print apron and carrying a mop. "Is Mrs. Mallard at home?" asked Hamish.

"I am Mrs. Mallard. What's up?"

Hamish judged Mrs. Mallard to be somewhere in her sixties. Surely a younger, stronger woman should have been chosen to foster the Palfour children.

"May I come in?"

She stood aside then led the way into a cosy living room. Hamish removed his cap and sat down. She seated herself opposite him and looked at him with mild, innocent eyes.

"Is your husband at home?"

"He's retired, but he does volunteer work in the charity shop. He's all right, isn't he?" she asked in sudden alarm.

"Yes, this is just a social call to see how the children are getting along."

Her face cleared. "Oh, they're just grand. We never had any children. Olivia and Charles are so good. I didn't think children were that polite and considerate these days. In fact, I could wish they were a bit noisier. But the school counsellor told me it would take them a long while to get over the shock."

Hamish left feeling uneasy. He could not banish the feeling that somehow Charles and Olivia were waiting for something.

■ ■ ■ ■

Fiona McBean was a classmate of Olivia's, and her parents were throwing a birthday party for her. To her dismay, her mother had insisted that she invite Olivia. "That poor lassie needs a bit of fun," said the mother. In vain did Fiona protest that Olivia gave her the creeps. But she brightened at the thought that Olivia did not socialise with any of them. She would be bound to refuse. To her dismay, Olivia politely accepted the invitation. Not only that, but with eyes full of tears, she asked if she could bring her brother as well. Startled, but suddenly compassionate, Fiona agreed. "My little brother, Harry, will be there and he's the same age as Charles so it'll be company for him."

Delighted, Mrs. Mallard raided her small savings account to buy a pretty party dress for Olivia, not realising in her innocence that girls were more apt to wear T-shirts and torn jeans than party dresses.

But Olivia thanked her sweetly, accepted a present of a Harry Potter book to give Fiona, and set off with Charles. She felt like a freak in her white dress. She wondered if very Protestant Mrs. Mallard had realised she had bought a confirmation dress.

At the McBean's, Olivia asked to use the bathroom. Once inside, she took off her coat, stripped off the dress, and put it in a bag after taking out jeans and a T-shirt. Then she went down to join the party.

At one point, she murmured to Charles, "They won't notice if you leave the room. Good luck!"

Charles was glad that the McBeans were the sort of parents who believed even sixteen-year-olds should be monitored at all times and had organised games for them all. Sixteen-year-olds in that part of the Highlands were still regarded as children.

Olivia hoped Charles would hurry because the party was rapidly dying, teenagers sulky at having to play stupid games. The party buffet was laid out in the adjoining room. Charles slipped out to where the bags he and Olivia had brought were in the hall. He took out a bottle of overproof Polish vodka, nipped into the dining room, and poured all the contents into the fruit punch before returning the empty bottle to his bag.

At the back of the house, across from the kitchen, was what Mr. McBean proudly called "my den." It was full of golfing trophies and old school photos. Charles quickly went through the desk until he found passports in the bottom drawer. He extracted Fiona's and Harry's and stuffed them in his pockets before slipping back into the party in time for the buffet.

At first the McBeans were delighted that their party seemed to have taken a lively turn as the children demanded more and more punch. But then they started fighting and throwing food at one another. Olivia and Charles slipped quietly away.

"Got them?" asked Olivia.

"Got them," agreed Charles.

Two days later, Hamish had an urge to go and look at the hunting box. The house looked square, grim, grey, and deserted. But as he climbed down from the Land Rover, he could hear the sound of a vacuum. He knocked on the door. After some time, Mrs. McColl answered it.

"Still working here?" asked Hamish.

"Aye, the lawyers have told me to keep the place clean until they decide what's to be done wi' the property. It's a funny thing. But I miss old Mrs. Colchester. She was right crabby but she always paid by the day. She would trundle her chair along to the strong room and come back with the money. She swore me and Bertha Dunglass to secrecy."

"But the key was lodged with the bank!" exclaimed Hamish.

"She didnae trust banks."

"Didn't you tell the Palfours this? Or the police?"

"She made us swear on the Bible. It doesn't matter now somehow."

"I don't remember there being any money mentioned in the inventory," said Hamish. "Did you ever see where she got the money from in the strong room?"

"No, we were never allowed to follow her when she went there."

Hamish stood deep in thought while Mrs. McColl looked at him impatiently. "Are ye going to stand there all day?" she asked at last. "I've got work to do."

"Aye, go ahead," said Hamish.

He took out his phone and scrolled down the numbers logged on it until he came to the lawyer's number and dialled. He waited impatiently to be put through to Mr. Strowthere. When he came on the line, Hamish asked, "When an inventory was taken of the strong room, was there any money there?"

"No, just the valuables."

Hamish thanked them and rang off. Had Fern and Ralph Palfour known about the extra key? But he could have sworn they were genuinely upset to find some of the valuables gone. Had Mary known? But if she had, she wouldn't have tried to blackmail Ralph Palfour.

Maybe Mrs. Colchester had only kept a purse in the strong room with just enough money to pay the cleaners.

Mrs. Mallard packed two suitcases for the Palfour children. A week before, they had given her a form to sign, allowing them to go on a school trip to Inverness and stay overnight. She told them to have a good time and waved them off.

The school counsellor had been off work with a bad cold. When she returned to work and switched on her computer, she found that everything on it had been wiped clean. The few children she had counselled were all interviewed except the Palfour children. She was told they were both ill and that Mrs. Mallard had sent a sick note.

She decided to call on them. She could not believe that a member of staff could have tampered with her computer. It couldn't be a virus. She had an excellent virus protector.

Mrs. Mallard looked surprised. "But they're not ill," she protested. "They've gone off on a school trip. They had a form for me to sign. A trip to Inverness with an overnight stay."

"There is no such trip," said Jane. "I'd better phone Hamish Macbeth."

Hamish cursed when he heard the news. He suddenly felt sure he knew where the money from the strong room had gone. An alert was put out for Olivia and Charles Palfour. Mrs. Mallard confirmed that both had passports and that their passports were missing.

Olivia and Charles settled back in their seats with sighs of relief on a Cyprus Turkish Airlines flight. They were travelling under the names of Fiona and Harry McBean. Fiona and Harry were black-haired and so they had dyed their hair black. "I nearly shat myself going through security in case they found the money," said Olivia. "But we got through. Thank goodness the money was still buried in the garden."

"Are you sure there's no extradition treaty with North Cyprus?" asked Charles.

"None. I checked."

Hamish went to see Jane. "Have you checked your credit card?"

"No, why?" she asked.

"If the Palfour children were using your computer, it could be to book plane or train tickets."

"They couldn't do that without my password. When I pay for anything online, my bank asks for a password to clear it."

"You don't keep a note of your password, do you?"

Jane blushed guiltily. "It's in my address book." She frantically began to search in her wallet. "My credit card's gone!"

"Phone your credit card people and see if anyone's been using it."

He waited while Jane phoned. He heard her exclaim after she had identified herself by answering a series of security questions, "Oh, no. That's awful. Someone has been using my credit card. Block it immediately." She rang off.

"Those villains!" she said to Hamish. "They booked two plane tickets on Cyprus Turkish Airlines."

"Under their own names?"

"No, under the names of Fiona and Harry McBean. They are pupils at this school."

"Get them in here!"

When Fiona and Harry came into the counsellor's office, Hamish said, "Olivia an

Charles Palfour are travelling under your names. Have you lost your passports?"

"You'll need to ask our dad," said Fiona. "He keeps them in his desk. Oh, the Palfours were at my birthday party last week."

Hamish asked them for their home address, left the school, and set off.

Mrs. McBean answered the door to him and looked shocked when he said that the Palfour children had probably stolen her children's passports. She hurried to her husband's desk only to confirm that the passports were gone.

Hamish phoned police headquarters and put out an alert for the two Palfours, this time under the names of Fiona and Harry McBean.

Jimmy phoned Hamish that evening to say that both had been on a Cyprus Turkish Airlines flight. There was no ex-tradition treaty with North Cyprus, but they had opened negotiations with the Turkish Cypriot government. "And that'll take forever," he said gloomily.

Hamish told him about the money from the strong room. "I wonder when they took it?" said Jimmy.

"I think that precious pair are more cold-looded than their parents. It wouldn't surprise me if they slipped into the strong room and helped themselves while everyone was out on the terrace, looking at the dead woman's body."

Olivia and Charles rented a small room in a back street in Kyrenia.

"The first thing we have to do," said Olivia, "is to pinch another couple of suitable passports. It's coming up to Christmas so there should be a good few tourists around. We don't want a couple who look like us. I need the passport of someone older and then I can disguise myself. With this black hair and a fake tan and some tarty clothes, I look a lot older. I'll get down to the Dome Hotel this evening. You'd better stay here. They'll be looking for a girl and boy. Scotland Yard have probably already got someone on the island looking for us."

"As long as Hamish Macbeth doesn't decide to come," said Charles. "I think that one can see through walls. I wish Andronovitch had got rid of him."

Olivia grinned. "All things are possible. I've got the Russian's number. He owes us."

"Too risky," said Charles. His face had gone wizened somehow, pinched with anxiety. "Have you got an e-mail for him?"

"Yes, we could send him a coded messag

281

His e-mail's registered under an alias. He called me Little Flower. There's an Internet café off the main drag. I'll try there. I'll log in a new mail account."

Olivia went down to the Dome Hotel that evening. She had returned to the cybercafé several times but there was no reply from the Russian. She had sent an e-mail saying, "Dear Daddy, Here in North Cyprus and need your help. Will be at the restaurant in the Dome Hotel in Kyrenia every evening. Little Flower."

She sat at her reserved table and looked around. The evening was mild and everyone was dining outside. A belly dancer was performing and a group of noisy English tourists was cheering her on.

Olivia scanned the room, looking at faces, noticing handbags. She felt suddenly uneasy. It was going to be more difficult stealing passports than she had imagined. She would need to wait until some of them got well and truly drunk.

A young man stood at the entrance, looking at a photograph of Olivia on his mobile phone. He had been warned she might have tried to change her appearance. But she had a black mole on her left cheekbone.

Then he saw Olivia sitting alone. Her

black hair looked as if it had been dyed and there was that mole.

He pulled up a chair at Olivia's table and sat down. "I am here to help you," he said in slightly accented English.

"That was quick," said Olivia.

"I was over on the Greek side when I got the message and came as quickly as I could."

"How did you find me?" asked Olivia.

"We have people who are good at finding out things. What is it you want?"

"My brother and I need two passports. We want to move on."

"That will cost you a lot of money."

"We have a lot of money."

He waved away a hovering waiter. "Then tell me where you are staying. That we could not find out. I will meet you there to arrange photographs and details at ten tomorrow morning."

Olivia surveyed him with her flat grey eyes. He was swarthy with black hair and dark eyes. Suddenly cautious, she did not want to meet him at their little flat. Better to meet them where there would be other people.

"We'll meet you here," she said, "in the bar."

He shrugged. "Okay."

He rose quickly and walked out of the restaurant.

Olivia and Charles were waiting in the bar, promptly at ten the following morning.

At ten minutes past ten, they were beginning to wonder whether he would show up when he appeared.

"I have to take you to a place to get your photographs taken."

Olivia hesitated, suddenly nervous, but Charles said, "Let's get it over with."

"First," he said, "I want twenty thousand pounds."

"I haven't got it on me," said Olivia. "If you wait here, I'll go and fetch it. Charles, you stay with him."

Olivia hurried back to the flat, unaware that she was being followed. She felt all-powerful and clever.

In the flat, she prised up two floorboards in the corner and lifted out a leather bag stuffed full of money and started counting out twenty thousand pounds. She did not hear the door opening. A sudden premonition of danger made her turn her head just as a strong arm came round her neck and a syringe was stabbed into her arm.

Charles looked at the man uneasily. Olivia

had been gone for an hour.

"I hope nothing has happened to your sister," he said.

Charles could not bear the wait any longer. With Olivia around, he felt older than his twelve years. Without his sister, he felt like a lost child.

"Let's go and see," he said.

It was a sunny day. Hard to believe it was winter. Charles mounted the staircase to the flat, shouting, "Olivia."

He stopped in the doorway, aghast at the sight of his sister's body before a man stepped from behind the door seized him and stabbed him with a syringe.

The two men who had attacked the Palfour children were in a casino that evening. They knew they would have to get the money they had recovered to Andronovitch, but both were gamblers and they were sure their boss didn't know the exact amount of the money. "Think they'll be all right?" asked one.

"Sure," said the other. "We'll ship them out at dawn."

Olivia recovered consciousness. She had been carrying a wad of notes taped to her body, so the syringe, plunged into the notes,

had only delivered a small amount of tran-
quilliser.

She was violently sick. Then she went to
her brother and tried to shake him back to
consciousness, but without success. She
suddenly thought of Scotland, of the security of school, of the fact that if she did not
move quickly then the men would be back.
She ran to the door. It was locked. She went
to the window overlooking the street and
screamed for help.

People stared upwards, then three men
came pounding up the stairs and broke
down the door. One called the police while
another called to women in the street to
come up and comfort Olivia.

They were taken to a hospital in Nicosia
where Charles had his stomach pumped
out. The news of their rescue went from In-
terpol to Scotland Yard and up to the
Highlands.

Hamish heard the glad news that the Palfour children would be returning to Scotland as soon as Charles Palfour had recovered. The men who had attacked them had
not been found. He wondered what awful
fate had been planned for them. Maybe the
men hoped to sell them on some sex market.

■ ■ ■ ■

A particularly cruel winter released its grip on the Highlands and the villagers of Lochdubh began to look forward to the short but welcome summer.

The Palfour children had escaped prosecution because Olivia said she knew that Andronovitch would come after them. They denied knowing anything at all about the murders. Hamish was sure they were lying, but they had received so much sympathy from the press that Daviot decided not to charge them. Charles and Olivia were back at school and living again with the Mallards. Olivia was studying hard for her final exams and planned to go to university. Hamish, on going to interview them, found them as flat-eyed and as unchildlike as ever.

Ivan Andronovitch, travelling as a German businessman called Hans Berger, had endured plastic surgery and by rigorous dieting had lost several kilos in weight. He was now tall, and thin, with a pale smooth face and a shock of grey hair. He wore blue contact lenses. He checked into the Tommel Castle Hotel. His quarry was Hamish Macbeth. He had enjoyed living in London and going to first nights and society parties. Hamish Macbeth was the one who had taken that all away and Hamish Macbeth was going to pay with his life.

The Russian had dressed in new heathery tweeds "to blend with the surroundings," as he thought, not knowing that he was the subject of great speculation amongst the staff.

Word of the stranger reached Hamish Macbeth. He felt a sudden odd feeling of apprehension. In his bones, he had always felt the case was not closed until Andronovitch was found. He had warned the Palfour children to be cautious.

He decided, without telling headquarters, to take the Palfour children up to the Tommel Castle Hotel to see if they recognised anyone. He said, "If you see anyone who looks like thon Russian or either of the men who attacked you, don't let it show."

With the Mallards' permission, he collected the children from school and drove them up to the hotel. He couldn't help hoping that Priscilla had made one of her lightning visits.

"Now, don't be nervous," he said as he drove them into the car park at the hotel.

Olivia looked at him with contempt. "I am not nervous," she said.

288

Both Palfours had fair hair once more and Hamish thought, as he had before, that with the fairness of their hair and their flat grey eyes and the whiteness of their skin, they looked like visitors from another planet. Olivia at almost seventeen could hardly be thought of as a child any more, although in her school uniform she looked younger than her years.

Mr. Johnson, the manager, said that no, Priscilla was not visiting, and yes, Mr. Berger was in the lounge.

Hamish took out a photo of Andronovitch and studied it. He then showed it to Olivia and Charles. "Just to refresh your memories. Now take a good keek round the door of the lounge and then let me know."

He waited impatiently in the reception area. Finally they joined him. "No," said Olivia, "nothing like him at all."

"Wait here," ordered Hamish. He looked into the lounge to where Berger sat by the fire, reading a newspaper. The man looked nothing like Andronovitch.

"False alarm," said Hamish, leading them out to the Land Rover. "I'll drop you home."

The Palfours waved him goodbye but did not go indoors. "It *is* him," said Olivia.

"Nothing like him," scoffed Charles.

"He must have had plastic surgery."

"How do you know?"

"He's got that ruby ring on his finger and that Rolex on his wrist, the ones he always wore."

"So why didn't you tell the police?"

"Because they'd just lock him up and with his contacts, I bet he would escape. I want to get him."

"How?" demanded Charles. "If he's found dead and we've been seen up there, guess who they're going to suspect?"

"Not us. We'll climb out tonight through the window. Mr. and Mrs. Mallard go to bed early and sleep like the dead."

"You've gone mad," said Charles. "You mean, we kill him and two of us drag the body out of the hotel?"

"No, silly. We've got to wait until he's outside. Get him somewhere we can't be seen."

"And he pulls out a gun and says, 'Bang! Bang! You're dead.'"

"Shut up. I've got an idea." Olivia's eyes flashed with rare animation. "The maids at the hotel are all done up in old-fashioned black dresses and caps. Snob appeal. I'll get a uniform down in Strathbane. The main thing is to search his room and get rid of anything lethal. Then we'll arrange a meet.

We'll need to wait until the weekend. We can't forge another sick note. The school wouldn't believe us."

"But the maids will question you."

"So? As long as I keep clear of that manager, I can just say I've been newly employed. I'll disguise myself."

Olivia, with her figure padded out under her uniform, her face padded, and wearing glasses, asked one of the Polish maids which was Mr. Berger's room. She had just seen him leaving the hotel. "It's thirty-three," said the maid, "but it's been cleaned."

"He wants me to fetch something. I've left my passkey at home. I'll bring it in tomorrow. Don't tell the manager."

"Here's mine," said the maid, "but bring it straight back. It's my tea break. I'll be in the kitchen."

"What's your name?"

"Maria."

Olivia went up the stairs and let herself into the room. Putting on a pair of latex gloves, she began a quick search.

She looked in frustration at the safe in the corner. She didn't dare break into it and alert the Russian. She searched through his wardrobe and found a gun in one of his pockets. She had checked the Internet for instructions on how to unload a gun. She emptied out the shells and put them in her pocket.

Now all she could hope was that he didn't have another weapon in the safe.

She went down the stairs, gave the passkey to the receptionist, and told her to give it to Maria.

Outside the hotel, she went across the moors at the back to where she had hidden a bag. She changed out of her disguise, packed it away, and put on her school uniform. She then walked to the main road where she had left her bicycle and set out for Braikie.

She went into a café and sent an e-mail to Andronovitch. "Need money. Meet me at the Fairy Glen tomorrow at midnight on the bridge. Little Flower."

Andronovitch cursed when he read the e-mail on his BlackBerry. Those devil's spawn somehow had penetrated his changed look and were no doubt after him for money.

He put the gun in his pocket, drove one of the hotel cars to the glen's parking lot, and made his way to the bridge.

It was a wild restless night with the wind soughing through the trees. He stood on the bridge and waited.

It was very dark, and black clouds were piling up against the moon. Two black figures appeared at the end of the bridge. "Come closer," he said. "Uncle Ivan is here to help you."

Charles and Olivia slowly approached. He took the gun out of his pocket, pulled the trigger, and with dismay heard it click uselessly on the empty chamber. With a shout of wrath, he ran towards them — and straight into the long sharp carving knife which Olivia plunged into his chest. He staggered past them, wanting to get to his car with blood pumping out of the wound in his chest. He only managed to reach the end of the bridge before collapsing, slumped over the guardrail.

"Get his feet and help me heave him over," said Olivia.

Together, they tipped the Russian into the pool. The rain began to come down in torrents.

"That should wash any forensic evidence away," said Olivia. "Thank goodness, Dad taught me to drive. I only hope he left the keys in the ignition."

They hurried through the increasing storm to the car. "The keys are there," said Olivia. "Let's go."

They left the car in the hotel car park and

walked out to a stand of trees on the road where they had left their bicycles. Then they headed off through the storm to Braikie, climbing up to their rooms at the back of the house.

"Funny," whispered Charles, calling at her room before going to sleep. "I don't feel a thing. What about you?"

"Nothing, either. I washed the carving knife and put it in the dishwasher."

Two days later, Mr. Johnson phoned Hamish. "You'd best get up here. Berger is missing. All his clothes and his passport are in his room."

Hamish and Dick drove up to the hotel. They inspected the room, Hamish beginning to feel uneasy. He called Strathbane and a search began for the missing "German businessman."

EPILOGUE

And the shore echoes the song of the
    kingfisher,
And the woods echo the song of the
    goldfinch.

                     — Virgil

Three days later, when a rare spring day of
warm sunshine bathed the Highlands,
Frank Shepherd, the ornithologist, decided
to visit the glen. The gift shop was closed,
and there were no cars in the car park.
Perhaps the tourists would come back
again, he thought, when all the fears of
murder had disappeared. But he was surprised there weren't a few ghouls around,
the kind of people who slowed down to rel-
ish the sight of bad car crashes.

He climbed over the turnstile and made
his way to the bridge. The peaty water of
the pool below sparkled like gold in the sun.
And then he caught his breath. There was a

magical flash of blue as a kingfisher flew out from under the willow tree. He took out his camera and waited. Suddenly he lowered his camera in alarm, for rising to the surface of the tranquil pool was a dead body.

It rushed into his mind that he would have to report it immediately. Police and forensics would arrive and all the mayhem of an investigation. He had taken out his mobile phone, but now he put it away and made his way down from the bridge to the pool. At the end of the pool the water swirled lazily over a rocky lip, where it cascaded down into another pool below. It was not a dramatic waterfall like the one on the far side of the bridge.

He took off his socks and shoes and waded into the water, which was shallow enough near the body and only came up to his knees. With a shudder, he propelled the swollen body to the lip of the waterfall and gave it one almighty push.

Almost in slow motion, the body hovered on the edge and then disappeared. He scrambled back to the bank. His heart was thudding. He put on his shoes and socks and hurried back to the car park. He looked around. No one was in sight.

It was only after he had driven several

miles out of Braikie that he began to wonder if he had been seized with temporary madness.

He thought of Hamish Macbeth and his gentle highland voice and had an urge to go to Lochdubh and confess his crime. But that would mean the original crime scene would have to be investigated and the kingfisher might leave.

Two weeks later, Hamish Macbeth received a call from Mrs. Mallard. "A man has called, a Mr. Templeton, who says he is a distant cousin of Mrs. Colchester. He is an American and wants to take Olivia and Charles to America. The lawyer says he has been checked out and he is who he says he is."

"And what do the Palfours say?" asked Hamish.

"They say they want to go with him."

"Is he there now?"

"Yes."

"I'll be right over."

Mr. Templeton was seated with Olivia and Charles in the Mallards' living room. He was a rubicund man in his sixties with snowy white hair and an American accent.

He rose and shook hands with Hamish, but said, "I don't know why Mrs. Mallard should call the police. I've been vetted and Charles and Olivia are willing to go with me. I've a pleasant property in Nantucket. I had been travelling in the Far East and only heard of what these poor children had been through when I got back to the States. I will take them back with me on vacation until any formalities are finalised."

Olivia, dressed in her school uniform, still looked younger than her years. She was behaving like a child, smiling shyly and yet showing more animation than Hamish had ever seen in her. Charles was also smiling and holding his sister's hand.

Hamish cynically noticed the thick gold watch on Mr. Templeton's wrist and his expensively tailored suit.

Still, he asked Olivia, "Are you sure you want to go?"

"Oh, yes!" they both chorused.

Mrs. Mallard rushed from the room. Hamish followed her and found her sobbing in the kitchen. "There, now," he said, putting an arm around her shoulders. "Maybe it's for the best."

She pulled herself together and said, "After all I've done for them! They won't even look at me now. Can't wait to get away. Not a word of thanks out of either of them."

"I'll just be getting Mr. Templeton's address," said Hamish. "I'd like to learn how they get on in Nantucket."

He obtained the address and left with the sound of the Palfours' happy laughter ringing in his ears.

The day after, Callum and Rory Macgregor decided to take their new toy sailing boat to the glen and sail it in the pool. They were delighted when it cruised across the pool like a real yacht, but cried out in dismay as it reached the lip where the pool went down into the lower pool. It sailed bravely right over the edge and disappeared.

"Quick!" said Rory. "Let's get doon there afore it goes right away."

They scrambled down the edge of the small waterfall and then stood stock-still with shock. A body was floating in the pool, revolving gently in the current.

Callum sat down on a rock and began to shiver. Rory took out his prized mobile phone and with shaking fingers dialled the police.

The investigation was long and rigorous. A washed-out passport in the man's pocket identified him as Andronovitch. An autopsy revealed that he had undergone expensive plastic surgery.

Who had done it? A rival drug baron?

Hamish began to think of Charles and Olivia. Andronovitch may have threatened them.

He went to see Mrs. Mallard. "They've left!" she cried. "He took them off to an apartment he keeps in London for a holiday. They went off, hanging on to him, and never looked back once."

"Did he leave you a London address or phone number?"

"I'll get it for you."

Hamish phoned Jimmy and suggested that Scotland Yard should send someone to interview the Palfours.

Jimmy agreed. Hamish waited impatiently all day for a result.

He phoned in the evening. "They said they had never been near the glen at all. Hamish, since we can't tell exactly when he was murdered although it probably was on the first day he went missing, they were asked what they were doing during the days and nights he had disappeared. It seems they can account for every minute of their time. Mr. Templeton appears to be very rich. He had been winding up his businesses in the Far East, mostly clothes factories in Taiwan. Those kids are going to have a life of luxury."

The Palfours arrived in Nantucket two weeks later. Olivia had asked if she could go to college and was told she could.

Their excitement grew as they drove up to the gates of an imposing mansion. There was a barrier to the entrance and an armed guard.

Olivia noticed uneasily that the property was surrounded by a high electric fence, plastered with warning signs.

"You have a lot of security, Uncle," she said. Mr. Templeton had told them to call him "Uncle."

"It's wicked world, Olivia, and I am a rich man."

The inside of the house looked a bit like early American railroad baron. The furniture was heavy and Victorian. The walls were wood-panelled. Blinds were drawn down on all the windows, cutting out the sunlight.

Their rooms were a further disappointment. Each was small with a hard bed, a wardrobe, and a bedside table on which lay a large Bible. Each had a small bathroom en suite.

A grim-faced servant told them to rest, and to present themselves in the dining room for dinner at seven o'clock.

Charles sat on the bed in Olivia's room. "This is creepy," she said. "What's with the Bibles? He didn't strike me as particularly religious in London."

"He can't live that long," said Charles, who considered all those in their sixties to be ancient. "We'd better find out if he's made a will. The house is right on the sea. We can go swimming."

Jimmy called on Hamish. "I've just found out more about this Mr. Templeton," he said. "He's some religious nut. He told his local church that he had invited two young relatives and was looking forward to educating them in the path of Jesus Christ."

Hamish grinned. "I'd give anything to be a fly on the wall when they get there and find out what they're in for."

In the gloomy dining room, Mr. Templeton beamed at them as a surly maid served them with undercooked hamburgers and french fries. "Your first taste of real American food," said Mr. Templeton.

"We have hamburger joints in Scotland," said Charles.

"Now, Charles, it is rude to contradict your elders."

"Yes, sir," said Charles, picking up his

knife and fork.

"Put down your knife and fork," said Mr. Templeton. "I will say grace."

And he did . . . on and on and on. By the time he had finished, Charles and Olivia had lost their appetites.

"Now, I have hired a tutor for you because the summer holidays are due to begin," said Mr. Templeton.

"Can I go for a swim after dinner?" asked Olivia.

"No, you may not. Young girls should not expose their flesh for all to see."

Prison would have been better than this, thought Olivia wildly.

She intended to plan some sort of campaign after dinner with her brother. But when the meal was finished, they trailed after Mr. Templeton to the drawing room, where he read them large extracts from the Bible.

They were finally dismissed, and the burly servant followed them up to their rooms and locked them in.

They found the next day a sort of torture. Their tutor was a reverend, a man with a dog collar from which his tall thin head popped out like a vulture. His name was Jeb Pratt, and the tutoring took the form of religious instruction.

Olivia managed to have a word with Charles when they were allowed out in the grounds in the afternoon for a walk with the servant-guard several paces behind.

"We've got to get out of here," whispered Olivia. "He's mad and he'll drive us both mad if this goes on. We've got to escape."

"We'll never get past the guard or that electric fence," said Charles.

"If we could get out of our rooms at night and find some way to sabotage the electric current, we could make it. At least we've still got our passports. I'll think of something."

That evening before dinner, rummaging through her luggage for some sort of tool, Olivia came across a half-used bottle of clear nail varnish. She put a small amount into the lock.

When the servant came to lock them in for the night, he found that the key to Olivia's door would not turn. "I'll get the locksmith around in the morning to fix that," he said.

Olivia sat on her bed and waited until two in the morning. Then she let herself out and went to Charles's room next door. To her relief, the key was in the lock. She shook her brother awake and said, "Let's go. We'll only take our backpacks."

They crept down the thickly carpeted staircase. "There's bound to be a fuse box somewhere," said Olivia. "Look for a cellar or basement door."

They found it at the back of the hall and crept down the stone stairs.

"There it is!" said Charles excitedly. "All I have to do is pull the switch."

He jerked it down and the light in the cellar went off. They felt their way to the stairs and across the hall. Olivia gently unbolted three bolts in the massive door and turned the key, glad that all had been well oiled.

"Wait!" she said. "We need money. Let's look at the desk in his study."

"Do we have to?" asked Charles. "Someone could find us any moment."

"We've got to," said Olivia firmly. "Come on."

In the top drawer of the desk, they found a bundle of hundred-dollar bills, which Olivia quickly stored in her backpack.

With beating hearts they made their way to a corner of the grounds. Nimbly they scaled the fence and disappeared into the night.

Hamish Macbeth heard the news of their

disappearance two days later. "Why did it take all this time to let me know?" Hamish complained to Jimmy. "And why did they run away? Too much religion?"

"We only just heard ourselves," said Jimmy. "Old Mr. Templeton thought he could catch them himself. He got a rocket from the FBI. You wouldn't think two Britishers could disappear just like that."

"They must have got hold of some money. Did Mr. Templeton say he was missing any?"

"No, but he's been subjected to a rigorous investigation. His house has been searched and his grounds dug up for bodies. The press have just woken up to the story here. The American papers have been interviewing people on Nantucket, and it does seem he was some mad religious freak."

"I somehow don't think they're dead," said Hamish. "I feel right uneasy about it all. I only hope they don't ever come back to Scotland."

"Why?"

"It's unfashionable to call folks evil these days but that's what I think they are."

"We'll see," said Jimmy. "But ten to one we'll never hear about them again."

■ ■ ■

In this he was wrong. A week later, the Palfours were in the headlines again. They had
surfaced in New York and had got a top
criminal lawyer to take their case pro bono.
They were suing Mr. Templeton for mental
cruelty.

The American newspapers and television
were full of the case. Hamish and Dick
watched them on the news, Olivia dressed
in a much younger fashion, holding her
brother's hand, and both looking the picture
of injured innocence.

At the end of the case, Mr. Templeton was
sued for two million dollars, the money to
be put into a trust for the Palfours' upkeep
and education. Olivia, now seventeen, was
considered old enough to look after her
brother.

Mrs. Mallard phoned Hamish. "The poor
wee lambs," she cried. "Do you think they'll
ever come back and see me?"

God forbid, thought Hamish, but he
hadn't the heart to destroy her illusions
about the Palfours. "I'm sure they'll be back
one day," he said.

He went up to the glen on a fine sunny
day. The tourists were back but not in the

numbers that had been there before. He leaned on the bridge and looked down into the pool, catching his breath as the kingfisher flashed across.

It was hard to believe that the tranquil setting had been witness to such violence. Poor Mary. Thief she might have been, but he hated to think of her poor body lying under the water. What an odd attraction she had been with those wide blue eyes, curvaceous figure, and that delicate scent she wore.

Back at the police station, he said to Dick, "I hope we can hang on here. They're still closing police stations all over the north."

"Och," said Dick comfortably, "let's not think about things that make us miserable. I'm going to sit in the garden. Coming?"

"I'll just take my beasties for a walk."

With Sonsie and Lugs at his heels, he strolled along the waterfront. Everything was back to normal. No press and very few visitors. Just the way he liked it. And yet, he could not feel the case was closed. He would always wonder if the Palfours had been responsible for the death of the Russian.

Angela Brodie came up to join him as he leaned on the waterfront.

"Nice that everything is back to normal,"

she said.

Hamish scowled at the blue waters of the loch. "I wish I could feel that. It's those Palfours. They're a loose end, and I don't like loose ends."

Olivia and Charles were at that moment talking about him. "When the holidays come around," said Charles, "why don't we take a trip to Scotland?"

"Bad idea," said Olivia. "I bet that policeman, Macbeth, suspected us. I know he did."

"What can he find out now?" asked Charles.

"Well, maybe, I'll think about it."

"Are you sure you aren't demonising them?" Angela was asking. "I mean, with parents like theirs and that abuse at the school they went to in England, they must have been a bit warped, but I'm sure that's all."

"I wish I could believe that."

Angela laughed. "Why don't you ask the fairies for help?"

"The horrible business all started with superstition," said Hamish. "If old Mrs. Colchester hadn't believed in fairies, she wouldn't have been tricked. She would never have taken her valuables down to the pool for Mary to collect. She would never have made that will."

"I'd better get home and get lunch on," said Angela.

Hamish watched her go and then turned back and looked at the loch. He said out loud, "Fairies, be damned. There are no such things as fairies!"

A sudden wind whistled down the loch, and black clouds streamed in from the west. Dust and debris scurried around his feet, making odd whispering noises. The air was cold.

Calling to his animals, he hurried back to the police station, went in, and slammed the door.

He was just putting the kettle on when Dick came in from the garden. "You should come outside," he said. "It's a grand day."

"Nonsense, it's just turned cold."

"Come out and see."

Hamish went out to the garden and looked over the hedge. The sky was blue and the sun shone down.

"If I were a religious man, I'd cross myself," he said.

"What's that?" asked Dick.

"Never mind," said Hamish Macbeth.

ABOUT THE AUTHOR

M. C. Beaton was born in Scotland and lives with her husband in a village in the English Cotswolds. She writes mysteries featuring Agatha Raisin and Hamish Macbeth, as well as an Edwardian detective series published under the name Marion Chesney. Ms. Beaton is also a film commentator on BBC television.

The employees of Thorndike Press hope you have enjoyed this Large Print book. All our Thorndike, Wheeler, and Kennebec Large Print titles are designed for easy reading, and all our books are made to last. Other Thorndike Press Large Print books are available at your library, through selected bookstores, or directly from us.

For information about titles, please call:
(800) 223-1244

or visit our Web site at:
http://gale.cengage.com/thorndike

To share your comments, please write:
Publisher
Thorndike Press
10 Water St., Suite 310
Waterville, ME 04901